THE
MAN FROM
SHADOW RIDGE
★ ★ ★
BROCK & BODIE THOENE

THE
MAN FROM
SHADOW RIDGE

★ ★ ★

BROCK & BODIE THOENE

BETHANY HOUSE PUBLISHERS
MINNEAPOLIS, MINNESOTA 55438

With the exception of recognized historical figures, the characters in this novel are fictional and any resemblance to actual persons, living or dead, is purely coincidental.

Published by Bethany House Publishers
A Ministry of Bethany Fellowship, Inc.
6820 Auto Club Road, Minneapolis, Minnesota 55438

Printed in the United States of America

Library of Congress Cataloging-in-Publication Data

Thoene, Brock, 1952–
    The man from Shadow Ridge / Brock Thoene & Bodie Thoene.
       p.   cm. — (Saga of the Sierras ; bk. 1)

    I. Thoene, Bodie, 1951–   . II. Title.
III. Series: Thoene, Brock, 1952–   . Saga of the Sierras ; bk. 1.
PS3570.H463S23 bk.1
813'.54 s—dc20
[813'.54]   89–18467
ISBN 1–55661–098–X   CIP

This book is dedicated
to the men of the Thoene clan—
Papa Gil, brother Jess,
sons Jacob and Luke,
who share with us a love of the West, past and present,
and to Talon Zachary,
whose timely appearance, like that of this book
foretells great things to come.

Books by Brock and Bodie Thoene

The Zion Covenant

Vienna Prelude
Prague Counterpoint
Munich Signature
Jerusalem Interlude
Danzig Passage
Warsaw Requiem

The Zion Chronicles

The Gates of Zion
A Daughter of Zion
The Return to Zion
A Light in Zion
The Key to Zion

The Shiloh Legacy

In My Father's House
A Thousand Shall Fall
Say to This Mountain

Saga of the Sierras

The Man From Shadow Ridge
Riders of the Silver Rim
Gold Rush Prodigal
Sequoia Scout
Cannons of the Comstock
The Year of the Grizzly
Shooting Star

Non-Fiction

Protecting Your Income and Your Family's Future
Writer to Writer

BROCK AND BODIE THOENE have combined their skills to become a prolific writing team. Bodie's award-winning writing of the Zion Chronicles and the Zion Covenant series is supported by Brock's careful research and development. Co-authors of Saga of the Sierras, this husband and wife team has spent years researching the history and the drama of the Old West.

Their work has been acclaimed by men such as John Wayne and Louis L'Amour. With their children, Brock and Bodie live on a ranch in the Sierras, giving first-hand authenticity to settings and descriptions in this new frontier series.

CHAPTER 1

Harness leather groaned as the weary horses leaned into the last steep climb before Granite Station. The wagon was heavily loaded with flour, beans, salt and seed. Two sleeping boys and a bolt of calico cloth completed the freight.

Tom Dawson looked like a man more at ease on the back of a green-broke Indian pony than holding the lines of a team of farm horses. His rugged, sun-browned face was creviced from the weather like the landscape. His dark brown eyes matched the color of the hair that straggled across his forehead from beneath a black broad-brimmed hat. His features had the lean, angular look of a man by no means settled into an easy life, but the small wrinkles at the corners of his eyes betrayed the fact that he smiled on occasion, too.

It was late, past dark already. Tom had expected to reach his stop for the night hours before. The Army quartermaster sergeant who was to have met Tom early that morning had not arrived until midafternoon. The sergeant had sent Tom off with the warning that the stagecoach from Keyesville had been robbed. All five passengers and the driver had been brutally murdered.

Now Tom wished he had camped on the flat along the banks of Poso Creek with other travelers who had stopped for the night. His wagonload of goods might be just as tempting as gold to outlaws hiding out in the lower reaches of the Sierras. Tom's Colt Navy revolver and his Sharps carbine lay within easy reach beside him on the wagon seat.

The lights of Granite Station finally appeared atop the rise. Their friendly glow could not come too soon to suit Tom; he urged the horses to quicken their pace the last mile up the hill.

Granite boulders lined the road. The full moon cast sharp shadows from the rocky outcroppings, every one suggesting a cavernous skull. The steep ascent forced travelers to slow down; it was a natural place for an ambush. Tom knew that blood had been spilled here before.

The treeless slopes around Granite Station marked the dividing line between the oak-covered foothills of the Sierras and the grassy plains of the valley below. What thin grass grew among the boulders hissed in a fitful east wind—the dry breeze of Indian Summer that promised no rain to relieve the parched earth, but foretold winter's approach just the same. Over the rustle, Tom could just make out the tinny sound of a banjo and an occasional raucous laugh.

A rustling sound closer at hand startled Tom out of his reverie. Turning suddenly, he saw his older nephew, Jed, blinking up at him from a tangled pile of calico.

"Hold on, boy, don't wrestle that cloth. Your ma will skin us both," Tom scolded.

"I'm sorry, Tom. I thought I was home to bed an' got to reachin' for a blanket," the sleepy voice replied.

"Just lay still a mite longer; we're almost to Granite." From the long sigh that replied, Tom knew that Jed had already rejoined his brother in slumber.

Good boys, both of them, eager to go with Tom on this three-day trip—and not complainers either. But the long delay and the dusty trip up from town had worn them out.

At last the team crested the hill overlooking the little stage stop nestled below. The horses drew the wagon up and stopped across the dusty roadway from the small clapboard building that served as restaurant, saloon, and hotel of dubious accommodations. Tom planned only to grain the horses and buy a meal for himself and the boys. They would sleep on their cargo under the stars and start on at first light.

Tom could hear voices and the artlessly strummed banjo from the saloon, but no one appeared from the barn to assist Tom with the harness. He decided to let the boys sleep until he had obtained their supper, so he chocked the wheels of the wagon with two rocks that lay near for the purpose and unhitched the team. He turned them into the common corral, noting the presence of the station-keeper's chestnut gelding and three other saddle horses unknown to him. Stowing the harness on a rack in the barn, Tom strode across the road.

The stage stop appeared to lean over him as he approached. Tom reflected that even in daylight it seemed to be bracing itself away from the downhill slope on which it perched.

The music stopped abruptly with a cry of "More whiskey!" just as Tom pushed open the door.

Three men sat playing cards at a table at the far end of the room. The station keeper propped his banjo against the stone fireplace and scurried behind the mahogany bar to oblige the demand for liquor.

"Howdy, Tom." The station keeper, a slightly built, balding man in his early sixties, addressed him by name. "You jest up from town?"

"Yup, Charlie. Running late and almost too tired to be hungry."

The enticing aroma of a pot of beans simmering on a cast iron hook in the fireplace made Tom's stomach rumble, giving a lie to his words.

"Reckon I will have some beans. And the boys will be waking up, now that their cradle's quit rocking."

"Heh! Cradle quit rockin'; that's a good one!" Charlie's wheezy laugh was interrupted by a growl from one of the card players.

"Whar's the whiskey? You old coot, ya gonna jabber all night?"

Tom's attention swung around to the three men at the table. The one who had just spoken was a stout, florid-faced man who mopped his forehead with a stained bandanna.

The two who flanked the speaker exchanged a furtive glance across the table; it went unnoticed by the red-faced man. One of these was lean and drawn-looking. His clothes, a faded, nondescript shade of gray, matched his hair. Even his face had an ashen cast. He watched the others with intense, dark eyes, saying nothing.

The remaining member of the group was the only one Tom knew. It was Byrd Guidett. A rough, loud bully of a man, Byrd was built like a miner—as thick through his chest as he was wide, with an enormous neck and massive shoulders. He wore his curly red hair long, and his reddish beard was untrimmed.

Byrd Guidett still claimed to be living by prospecting for gold in the high reaches on the Kern, but it was said that he more likely worked the left side of law rather than the left side of a sluice box. A mining partner of Guidett's had disappeared in a mysterious accident, and since then respectable folks had tried to walk the long way around Byrd.

"Drink up, ol' cuss," Byrd said. "Maybe yer luck will change." This was addressed to the stout man who had poured two fingers of rotgut into his glass and the other two on the table.

Charlie scampered back to the fire and, taking three none-too-clean tin plates off a sideboard, dished up three helpings of beans. He added a handful of corn-dodgers to each plate and passed the lot to Tom.

"What do I owe you?" asked Tom.

"Did ya bring my coffee?" asked Charlie. At Tom's nod, he added, "Well, if ya don't charge for freightin' my arbuckle, I reckon a few beans and 'pone is free."

"Well, much obliged, and welcome to boot." Tom started out, then stopped short at a movement in the corner behind the card players. He had been wrong about there being only four occupants of the dimly lit room, for crouched on the floor near the sweaty-browed gambler was a small Negro boy. At Tom's sudden stare, Charlie's gaze also moved to the boy, and then catching Tom's eye he shook his head slowly as a warning to say nothing.

"I'll come out directly to see to yer team," Charlie said.

With a slight narrowing of his eyes and a quick nod, Tom left with supper for him and the boys.

The boys roused themselves and eagerly lit into the beans. Because they were still nine parts tired, the boys' usual banter was absent, and they ate in silence. Presently, the saloon door opened and Charlie came across to join them. The flickering pale light that came out through the wavy glass panes gave only enough illumination for Charlie to see the questioning look on Tom's face.

"I'm glad you said nothin', Tom. That's two powerful mean men in there. Byrd you know of, and that fat Missouri fella's been yellin' at me since he an' the boy came."

When Tom made no reply, he went on. "Byrd an' that gray-lookin' fella rode in about sundown. The Missourian was already pretty likkered up, an' they got this game goin' right away like they was anxious to get started."

"How do you know the one's from Missouri?" asked Tom.

"Well, he tol' me he come from there with his *chattel*. I ain't seen no cows and then he says he means the little colored bas—" At Tom's sharp look he left the word unfinished.

"A black man? Can we see 'im?"

"No, boys, it isn't our affair. And anyway it's just a child."

Charlie resumed. "So them three been playin', with the pike drinkin' and losin' and Byrd winnin', and the slim fella jest watchin'."

"Obliged for the beans and the word," said Tom. "Guess we'll turn in now." The boys started a groan of protest, but fell silent at a look from their uncle. He handed the plates over to the station keeper. "I'll put out some grain for my team if it's all right."

"Help yerself, Tom, and g'night to y'all." Charlie moved back across the road, dropping a tin plate in the process. He appeared to inspect it briefly by the window's glow; then wiping it on the seat of his denim pants, he seemed to find it satisfactory and went in.

The shot and the crashing noise came just before dawn. Tom's mind instantly sprang awake. Grabbing the Colt Navy he ordered, "Jed! Nathan! Get in the barn and stay there!"

Crouched beside the wagon, he waited till the boys had sprung over the side and run into the barn's opening. For a moment he thought an extra shadow ran after them, but the moon had set and he shook his head to clear his vision. His attention was turned to the saloon as the door burst open and Byrd thrust himself out.

"Whar's 'at nigger? He's mine now. Whar'd he go?" Byrd moved forward as if to cross the street and enter the barn. "I'll bet he run in here!"

The click of Tom's .36 caliber as he cocked it was loud enough to be heard in the moment Byrd paused for breath. He froze in his tracks, as did the gray man who had appeared in the doorway behind him.

Slowly Byrd turned to face Tom. "What's this all about?" Tom asked quietly, but with an unmistakable edge to his voice.

"I won that nigger fair an' square, and that hunk of lard called me a cheat an' made to draw on me!"

"So you shot him," said Tom.

"It was a fair fight, wasn't it, Yance?" This last was addressed over his shoulder to the man in the doorway.

"Yup, I seen it all."

"So move outta my way," ordered Byrd with a new burst of bravado. "He's mine an' I aim to fetch him!"

"California's free territory," replied Tom softly, "so you can't *own* him. Anyway," he added, "I was right here and I didn't see him go into the barn."

"I mean to look—" Byrd began, then stopped as Tom raised the pistol to point directly at Byrd's chest.

"Nope," Tom said. "He's probably scared and still running over these hills. Besides, if you were to find him, he'd have to be held for the inquest."

Yancey started, then said, "Byrd, we don't need no inquest."

"Shut up!" Byrd snorted. Facing Tom, he added, "Yer prob'ly right about the kid. He lit a shuck out the door and he's maybe halfway back to Missouri by now." Raising his hands, open-palms toward Tom, he began to back slowly toward the saloon. "We've wasted enough time here already. If a deputy wants a statement, he can look us up. *Charlie* will say what happened, won't ya, *Charlie*?"

The old station keeper cleared his throat nervously from inside the doorway. Taking this noise to mean *yes*, Byrd added, "Bring our winnin's, Yance. I'll get the horses."

Tom watched in silence without uncocking the revolver as Byrd retrieved two bridles from the corral posts and caught his and Yancey's horses.

Charlie came out, and at a nod from Tom, entered the barn to return with two saddles and blankets. Moments later, Byrd and Yancey were mounted. As they settled into their high-cantled saddles, Byrd rode slowly over to Tom.

"I won't forget ya, Tom Dawson," he said; then he and Yancey spun their horses and loped up the road to the northeast.

CHAPTER 2

Tom stood watching the two ride out of sight. He thought it wise not to let down his guard too quickly, so he called out, "Charlie, do you still have that shotgun back of the bar?"

"Why sure I do, Tom!"

"You'd best bring it out here."

It was only after Charlie had returned with an ancient but serviceable double-barreled shotgun that Tom allowed his attention to turn from the knoll over which Byrd and Yancey had ridden.

"You'd better keep watch till full light," Tom directed the station keeper.

" 'Deed I will! This here load o' buck is good for polecats and other varmints—even birds!"

Tom entered the dark stable softly and called to the boys.

"Jed, Nathan. Come on out now, boys; it's all over." A rustling of hay greeted his ears; then two tousled and straw-covered heads appeared from under the hay mow.

"We heard it, Tom."

"But we was real still."

"I know, boys. You did real well."

"Can *he* come out now, too?" asked Jed, the older boy.

17

"What? He who?"

"You know, the little black'un!"

So there really had been a third boy-sized shape that darted into the barn! In protecting his own nephews, Tom had aided the child in staying out of Byrd's clutches as well.

"Come out and show yourself, boy. No one will harm you now."

A further rustling and a third hay-strewn head poked up. Only the outline of a round dark shape could be seen. Tom stepped to a post and took down the lantern; then reaching into his pocket, he extracted a Lucifer match and proceeded to light the lamp.

"Come on out, boy. Let's have a look at you."

At this further reassurance, the child stood up and brushed himself off, then took a place beside Nathan. The boys were almost identical in size. Both wore overalls, but the black child wore no shirt, and his clothing was ragged, here and there inexpertly mended. Both boys were barefoot. Tom stooped to nine-year-old height and asked gently, "Do you have a name, child?"

"Yassuh, massah. I be Montgomery James," he said with a shy grin.

"Well, Montgomery, you need not call me massah— nor anyone else. California is a free state."

The boy's eyes grew wide and round with wonder. He had run to escape the shooting that had killed his former owner. He had not thought of running from slavery to freedom.

"Please, suh, where does I go den?"

"Well, now, child, where are you from? Do you have family or kin?"

The boy looked troubled. His grin faltered, and he

replied, "I reckon not, suh. Mistuh James, he the one what was shot, taken me off'n de farm when I was real small. I disremember any folks—"

"How do you come to be in California?"

"Mistuh James, he be a Missouri man. After order eleben come, he in trouble wid de sol'jers, an' we come away real sudden-like."

"All right, Montgomery, that will do for now. Let's get you three some breakfast. It will soon be light enough to travel and I'm anxious to be home."

While the boys hastily washed their hands and faces in the horse trough, Charlie set down the shotgun long enough to bring out more cornbread cakes and a clay jug of buttermilk. By this time the first rays of dawn had risen over the eastern hillside above the little stage stop.

The boys ate while Tom and Charlie held a conference over the Missourian's body.

"I'll help you bury him, Charlie."

"Obliged to ya, Tom. I'll fetch the shovels."

Tom leaned over the dead gambler and absently poked through his pockets. A handful of silver coins, a handkerchief, and a single cuff link engraved "J.D." Tom straightened up as Charlie entered the room carrying two shovels.

"Hadn't we best bury him outside, Charlie?" suggested Tom dryly.

"Laws yes! Killin's fluster me so," Charlie stammered. "Here, hold these." He threw the shovels to Tom. In the moment's confusion, Tom put the handkerchief and coins on the bar, but slipped the cuff link into his pocket. Leaning the shovels against a wall, Tom grasped the feet and Charlie the arms of the corpse as they half carried, half dragged it outside. Wrapped in an old canvas slicker, the body soon lay beside four other earthen mounds on the slope a short distance below the stage stop.

"You don't worry about planting them too deep, do you?" remarked Tom.

"Naw, some kin may want to claim 'em, and then I'd jest have to dig 'em up again."

The two men walked back up the hill to where Jed and Nathan had harnessed the team and hitched them to Tom's wagon. The boys had already rejoined the freight in the wagon bed, but Montgomery James stood uncertainly alongside the rear chestnut's flank.

"What'll ya do with the black child, Tom?" inquired Charlie.

"Me?" asked Tom, startled. "I thought you'd keep him here with you."

"Naw, Tom, naw. I've got to send word to the sheriff about the killin' by the afternoon coach. I can't watch him, less'n he run off. He's a witness, ya know, and contraband to boot."

"Charlie, he has no place to run *to*. Besides, I thought I left all that contraband talk behind when I left . . ." Here Tom's voice trailed off as if he had gotten dangerously close to a topic better left alone.

"Please, Uncle," begged Jed, "let's take him home with us. Ma will look after him, and he won't run away from us, will you, Mont?"

"Now, boys, I don't want to impose on your mother without asking."

Charlie interrupted this objection by saying, "Why sure. What's one more young'un, more or less? He won't eat much, and I can tell the sheriff whar to find him."

Tom gazed down at the tight black curls and fearful

eyes upturned to search his face, and sighed, "All right, child. Climb aboard."

"Oh no, suh. I nevuh rides *wid* no white folks—I jes' walks alongside."

"Well, Montgomery, if you are to be staying with us for a time, you'd best get in. We don't make our *guests* walk, whatever color they may be."

Urged on by the boys already seated in the wagon, Montgomery climbed over the tailgate and sat down on a flour sack. An unexpected smile broke over his face as though he had just seen a glimpse of heaven.

Tom climbed up, and with a nod to the gnarled station keeper to unblock the wheels, Dawson slipped the brake lever and clucked to the team.

"Be seein' ya, Tom—best be right wary now," the old man urged.

Without a reply except a pull on the brim of his hat to acknowledge the advice, Tom started the wagon out of Granite Station and up the hill toward home.

The journey was a familiar one to the team, and they needed little direction or encouragement from Tom. They stepped out smartly, confident that their home pasture lay at the end of one more day's pull. The ease of travel allowed Tom to review the night's events. He did this with a part of his mind while at the same time remaining vigilant. He thought it unlikely that Byrd would seek vengeance openly on an obviously prepared foe, but the possibility of an ambush remained. Byrd's personality ran to open force if he clearly had the upper hand, but to treachery if he didn't.

Tom mused that the Missourian's destiny to die by gunfire seemed foreordained. If it were true that he had recently left his native state, then he could have only just escaped the same fate as at the station. The Missouri-Kansas border was on fire. Pro-slavery and abolitionist factions raided each other's settlements with bloody results.

In fact, the bloodiest of all these clashes had just occurred in August in the sleepy little Kansas town of Lawrence. Quantrill's Confederates had swept into Lawrence, overpowered its inhabitants, and slaughtered three hundred men and boys while putting much of the town to the torch.

The reports of such sickening atrocities carried out against innocent civilians had accelerated since the outbreak of the Civil War, but the turmoil had existed since the early 1850s. Pro-slavery elements from Missouri had sought to force their views on the newly organized Kansas territory. Abolitionist leaders like John Brown had responded with "an eye for an eye." And so it had gone.

The eastern half of the nation was embroiled in war, to be sure, but Kansas and Missouri seemed to be engaged in a blood feud, a duel to the death liable to end only with the destruction of *all* the participants.

Tom pivoted around to look at the boys in the wagon bed. Montgomery seemed to have overcome his shyness, and all three boys were talking animatedly and, glory be, comparing skin colors! He was pleased that Jed and Nathan showed no distaste for the black child, but rather a frank and open curiosity. Just now, Montgomery was elaborating on his departure from Missouri.

"An' de gen'rl, he says dat de country is lousy wid rebs. So he give out wid order 'leben. Ever'body got two days to move! Ever'body in a tizzy, throwin' things out de windas into dere wagons an' such. But Mistuh James, he catch wind dat de sol'jers comin' to arrest him. So we dasn't wait, but lit out!"

Tom resumed his thoughts. Just such turmoil had caused him to leave Missouri himself two years before. In 1861, he had been a member of the Marion Rangers, a Missouri regiment. The regiment's pro-Southern loyalty asserted itself, and the Rangers decided to join the Confederacy. Tom had no stomach to fight on behalf of slavery, but to reenlist in a Union outfit would force him into battle against former friends and neighbors. Maybe he had been wrong not to stand up for his belief in the Union, but he had been grateful when word had come from his brother Jesse.

Tom had mixed feelings about joining Jesse; after all, other issues were involved. . . . But at last he had decided to go.

For two years, things had been peaceful in California, and the war only a distant tragic noise. Others from the Ranger group had made the same choice to come west. He had even had a letter from a former comrade-in-arms, Sam Clemens, late of Missouri, now living in Virginia City, Nevada territory.

Tom sighed. Despite what the quartermaster sergeant had said, he hoped the raid on the gold shipment was only robbery and murder and the connection to the rebel cause just a ruse. He didn't want to think that this peaceful countryside would experience the horror of Civil War, even though he knew that there were Southern sympathizers among the hill folk.

The wagon was rounding an oak-covered hillside on the last level stretch before the climb up Pruitt's Hill when Tom saw a flash ahead and just to the right of the wagon road. A gun barrel?

Tom slowed the team and cautioned the boys to be ready to jump behind a nearby clump of rocks if need be. He checked the loads in the Sharps and the Colt, then watched carefully the spot where he had seen the flash. There it was again, nearer the road this time. It appeared to be on the fork in the trail that led eastward to Poso Flat and the gold fields beyond.

The ears of the chestnuts were pricked forward, standing at attention.

In the next moment, horses and driver relaxed as the approaching sounds indicated that their maker had no sinister purpose. Muleback, with sunlight flashing from his spectacles, and singing "Old Hundred," Parson Swift rode into view.

"Hello, Tom," he called.

"Hello, Parson," Tom returned as he waited for the man of God to approach.

"Well, hello to you also, boys, and—saints alive, who's this?"

Briefly Tom explained Montgomery James's presence and the events of the shooting.

Parson Swift nodded gravely. "That explains why Byrd passed me by without a word a while back. He and a man I didn't know were riding down into Poso Flat just as I was starting up the grade. I'm heading down into the valley for a spell. I'll stop by Granite and say a few words over the man."

"I'm sure his family, if he had any, would be grateful," said Tom. Then he added, "And I'm glad Byrd's heading off east away from our track. I didn't want to see these youngsters involved in a gun battle."

"Amen, and you remember, young Tom Dawson, those that live by the sword will die that way." The lanky parson started his mule toward the valley, and the four in the wagon made their way home in the drowsy after-noon.

————

When the fork in the road leading to the town of Greenville appeared, Tom urged the team past it and on toward home. Shortly thereafter, they came to the ford of the Poso known as Laver's Crossing.

Shadow Ridge, which now loomed directly ahead, was aptly named. Its chaparral and oak-covered sides never appeared distinct to the eye, but were always hazy, as though enveloped in a thin blue smoke. Local Indian lore had it that the mountain was sacred; some said haunted. It was called a "ghost mountain" because it was a perfect mirror image of the Sierra Nevada peak some ten miles due east.

While the eastern range reached up to cedars and pines, it was crisply outlined against the sky. Shadow Ridge, though real enough, had a mirage-like quality. The Tuolomne elders maintained that Shadow Ridge was home to "shadow animals" and other spirits, coun-terparts of the real deer and grizzly bears that made their homes in the Sierras. All the tales made good sto-rytelling material for gusty nights around a crackling fire. The trails of the Tuolomnes and Yokuts skirted the base of the peak without venturing into its precincts, but their fear had not bothered Tom's brother Jesse at all.

Jesse had brought his wife and two young sons to the property he homesteaded on the eastern slope of Shadow Ridge. His land ran from a lower oak-covered ridge down to the fertile plain watered by Poso Creek. Quail and gooseberries flourished in abundance on the hillside, while the bottom land furnished feed for cattle and good soil for planting.

Jesse's Missouri upbringing made him feel more at home as a farmer than a rancher, and his expertise soon paid off. With the army's presence at Fort Tejon and the San Joaquin Valley too swampy and malarial for farming, he rightly judged that in his corner of this mountain valley, potatoes would grow well—and travel well, too.

He had made enough money to pay for sawn cedar to build a fine home for his family, and his success with the army contract had prompted him to invite his brother to join him.

The team turned into the lane leading to the barn. Jed and Nathan jumped off before it had completely stopped, and ran to where their mother was tending her pumpkin vines in the little kitchen garden.

"Ma, can Montgomery stay with us?"

"He doesn't have any kin, but now he's free!"

"We don't have to send him away, do we?"

"Now, boys, what's all this about?" Emily asked, waiting for the flow of words to slow and a coherent explanation to emerge.

Tom lifted Montgomery down from the wagon bed. The black child trailed behind as Tom left the team standing patiently and walked over to his sister-in-law.

" 'Lo, Emily," Tom began. He felt shy in approaching, not because he doubted her kind heart, but because he was always cautious to be extra polite to his brother's wife. Tom and Jesse had been rivals for Emily's attention in Missouri. Jesse had pressed his suit and won because he had been able to present his plan for a home, a farm, and a life, while Tom had still been devil-may-care— attractive as a dashing beau but not serious enough for a prospective husband. Tom believed that Emily cherished him still, but their affection was of the purest and deepest kind now.

She stood in her garden, dressed in dark blue calico, with her fine honey-blond hair escaping the bonnet she wore to protect her face. The afternoon sun lit up her pert nose and creamy skin. Tom began again.

"Montgomery here"—he turned to beckon the child to come and stand beside him—"is an orphan. He was brought to California by a Mr. James, who got himself killed by Byrd Guidett last night. Byrd was going to take him away, but Montgomery, well, Mont doesn't need to *belong* to anyone now. Anyway, can he stay on the place for a time?" he concluded lamely.

"Of course he can, and he's welcome! Byrd Guidett is nothing but a cut-throat and a thief. Come here, Montgomery." Her beauty and easy manner won the child's heart in an instant, and he crossed to stand beside Nathan.

"Will you look at that? You two boys are the same size. Montgomery, I'll bet we can find some of Nathan's clothes that will fit you, and I'm sure he'd enjoy your assistance with his chores."

"Yessum. I'se a hard worker an' don' eat much," responded Montgomery.

"You shall eat your fill, for we've plenty and to spare. After"—she addressed herself firmly to all three youngsters—"you've washed up. I declare, you've brought home another forty acres on your faces."

"C'mon, Mont, I'll race you to the pump!" shouted Nathan as all three raced off around the corner of the house.

"Mind, now, wash those arms and necks, too," she called after them.

"Yes, Ma," and "yessum" blended together, floating back over their retreating forms.

She turned to regard Tom with an upraised eyebrow. "Was there trouble for you, Tom?" she inquired.

"Not to speak of. Byrd and his partner backed down pretty easy. I thought there might be mischief on the road, but Parson Swift said he saw them headed down Poso Flat way. Anyway, Byrd wasn't anxious to wait around for an inquest into the shooting."

"Is Jesse around?" he continued.

"No, but I expect him back most any time. He finished the work on the barn roof and went off to hunt some quail. You should wash up, too; supper's almost ready."

"I'll just unload the wagon and see to the team, and then I'll be along." They parted toward barn and house— the slim, wiry, dark man and the slender, fair woman.

Jesse appeared in the barn just as Tom was hanging up the harness. The family resemblance could be seen in their faces, but Jesse was broader and just a shade taller. His serious face showed lines of concern.

"Byrd Guidett again?"

"Yes, and a killing this time." Tom related the story to his brother, then went on.

"What's more, the stage was robbed south of Wheeler Ridge early yesterday. Everybody was gunned down."

"Did they try to make a fight of it?"

"No, and that's the worst. They were lined up beside the road and shot down in cold blood. The army thinks it's the work of reb agents who would be recognized hereabouts."

"Could that be Byrd's doing too?" asked Jesse.

"He's capable of it. Charlie said Byrd and his partner seemed anxious to settle in to a card game, like they'd nothing better to do and no hurry to be elsewhere."

Jesse added, "They could have stashed the gold somewhere, and then wanted to throw off suspicion by being purposefully seen a good distance from the killing."

"If that's so, Byrd's greed and temper may have messed up his plan. If he had the drop on that James fellow, he should have left off without another killing."

"Maybe we should share our thoughts with the sheriff."

"I was thinking that very thing. If we ride over to Greenville tomorrow, maybe Deputy Pettibone will be around to listen."

CHAPTER 3

The Dawson brothers had done well in their sale of the potato crop to the Union soldiers of Fort Tejon. A neat stack of twenty double-eagle gold pieces glistened on the table between them.

"When you're done admiring the profits," Emily joked, "I'll deposit those in the bank if you don't mind."

The Dawson "bank" consisted of a loose stone in the fireplace and a quart canning jar half full of assorted coins and a few gold nuggets that served as small reminders that Jesse had once dreamed of striking it rich in the gold fields. They had long since found contentment in the wealth of healthy sons, a good crop, plenty to eat and an occasional bolt of calico. It was *enough*. Jesse had come to believe that a man who wasn't satisfied with enough would never have enough to be satisfied.

Tom had dreamed of a different kind of gold mine, a different way to strike it rich. Now, as Emily scooped the meager stack of gold coins into the jar, Tom's eyes glistened with amusement.

"Wait a minute," he said, raising a hand laconically. "That's not all."

"Not all?" Jesse leaned forward. "That's more than I expected."

Tom nodded. "For the potatoes yes." He reached into the deep pocket of his jacket and pulled out a leather bag that seemed to bulge at the seams. He hefted it twice for the effect of its weight. Emily blinked in astonishment and then looked from Tom to Jesse, then back to Tom again.

"The horses?" Jesse croaked.

Tom grinned broadly and nodded, tossing the bag onto the table with a heavy thud. "In advance."

"But they're not even broke yet!" Emily exclaimed.

"It doesn't matter." Tom took the jar from her and placed it beside the leather lump on the table. "It seems Mr. Lincoln's army is desperate for our horses."

"But they're only a scruffy bunch of mustangs," Jesse protested.

"Doesn't matter to the army anymore. I told you, for every man that falls in that cursed war, ten horses go down. Some to rifle fire, some to artillery, some to the stew pot of hungry men. North and South, the armies are all afoot now."

Emily furrowed her brow. "And they should stay afoot, too, if it makes it harder for them to kill one another."

In reply, Tom upended the sack, letting a heap of gold coins clatter to the table top among the cups and saucers. "That is not the opinion of the Union army, Emily."

She gasped at the sight. "If Mr. Lincoln would pay that in advance for wild, hook-nosed creatures that his officers have never seen, then he is a fool, indeed!"

"The South would pay that much for them as well," Tom shrugged. "Maybe more."

Jesse picked up a double-eagle and held it to the

light. "Then Jefferson Davis is a fool, too."

"I won't argue with that," Tom nodded. He scooped up a handful of coins. "Two thousand dollars here." He paused for effect. "And this is only half of it. "Another two thousand when we deliver forty green-broke horses to the Union army at Fort Tejon."

Jesse gave a low whistle. "A hundred a head?"

Tom produced a neatly folded paper, emblazoned with the official seal of the Union army. "I wasn't expecting more than twenty apiece."

Emily leaned over her husband's shoulder and scanned the document. "They want the horses in a month!" she exclaimed. "But you haven't even started to break them!"

There had been nearly fifty horses corralled in five makeshift corrals since mid-July. Two journeys into the Mojave desert had yielded the half-starved mustangs for Jesse and Tom. Emily had shook her head in disapproval at the sight of the bunch and had proclaimed that no one in his right mind would mount an animal so homely, let alone spend good dollars to buy one. She had resented the feed that had disappeared down their ungrateful gullets, but after a month of good Dawson hay, she admitted that they looked a bit healthier.

"Only a month, you say?" Jesse clutched her hand and winked. "Why, I've tamed wilder things in half a day."

She blushed and turned toward the stack of dishes on the kitchen counter. "Not *forty* mustangs!"

"You'll just have to get a bigger jar for the bank, Emily," Jesse chided. "And have little faith."

"Just don't go get yourselves all busted up. You're not eighteen anymore, you know."

Tom leaned back in his chair with the casual air of a man who had won a great victory. "We're not going to break 'em," he teased. "We'll put Jed and Nathan and Montgomery to the chore."

Emily narrowed her eyes and threatened him with a swat from her dishcloth if he talked any more nonsense. "Food for the stomachs of Union soldiers," she muttered. "And now food for Southern cannons! I thought we were supposed to be far away from this war."

―――――――

Dinner that night was a sumptuous affair, planned as a celebration for the successful sale of the potato crop to the army.

Emily had prepared a turkey, shot by Jed and proudly carried back to the farm by him from a manzanita thicket. She had stuffed it with cornbread and sunflower-seed dressing, lightly spiced with fragrant sage. For the cornbread that accompanied the turkey there were gooseberry preserves and honey from their own hive of bees. A bowl of boiled potatoes brought good-natured groans from the table; but with a topping of fresh butter, salt, and a dash of red pepper, they disappeared as quickly as the rest.

Montgomery had to be coaxed to join them at the table, but once in place, he began to eat with as much enthusiasm as the others.

The conversation was of the most pleasant variety. They talked of how the money would be spent—so much for staples, so much for a new three-row cultivator, some for household furnishings and "frippery," as Jesse joked with Emily.

"That quartermaster sergeant said that next year

they could take as many more loads as we could send," said Tom.

"That so? Well, it sounds like we'll need that cultivator real soon. We can open up that lower quarter section a year sooner than I expected," thought Jesse aloud.

"The sergeant told me they were getting another complement of troops to patrol the desert country clear to the Colorado."

Jed spoke up. "Yes, and he said they'd be riding camels, just like the wise men did—you know, for crossing the sand."

Nathan broke in, "With one big hump and a long snaky neck. The sergeant said they can spit tobacco juice fifty yards right in a fella's eye!"

"Now, boys," Jesse admonished, "you mustn't believe all you hear. That man was just funning with you."

"Yes, sir, Pa," replied Jed, while Nathan still looked stubbornly committed to the truth of his tale.

"But he said we'd see 'em."

"That will be enough, Nathan," Emily reproved. "Mustn't argue with your father." Then hastening to make sure no one felt too chastised, she asked, "Who's ready for pie?"

Vigorous nods of assent went around the table, and Emily retreated to the kitchen and returned moments later with a fresh baked apple pie, its flaky crust laced with sugar and cinnamon. "Now, just wait till I give you some more coffee, and then I'll dish it up."

As she completed a circuit of the table and prepared to serve the pie, Tom interrupted by getting to his feet. Raising his coffee cup he began, "Gentlemen, I give you the lady of the feast. A toast to Emily."

All the males rose, even Montgomery, who after a

moment's uncertainty, grabbed his glass of milk, as did Jed and Nathan. "To Emily," said Jesse and Tom.

"To Ma," echoed Jed and Nathan.

"To Missy," added Montgomery.

Emily blushed and smiled, obviously pleased at the tribute.

As they seated themselves again and Emily began passing the pie around, Jesse observed, "Yes, sir, Tom, right here's what a man works for. A fine family and the means to feed and shelter them. A fine wife who makes a man look forward to coming home to supper. You know, Tom, you need to get married. There's nothing like it in the whole world."

———

After the meal the men sat smoking their pipes while Emily knitted. They had drawn their chairs up to the fireplace more for sociability than for warmth. The oak log glowed pleasantly. The three boys could be heard talking and occasionally laughing in the kitchen. Presently they finished washing the dinner dishes and came to stand in a row beside the scrubbed oak dining table.

Tom leaned forward to knock the dottle out of his pipe into the stone fireplace and stood up. "Mont, I expect you can bunk with me. Emily, that was as fine a meal and as enjoyable an evening as could be found anywhere. Good night Jesse, Jed, Nathan."

"G'night, Missy; I nevuh et bettah," added Montgomery.

"You are most welcome, both of you. Montgomery, we are pleased to have you stay with us. You must remember in your prayers tonight to thank God for your deliverance. And you, boys," addressing Jed and Nathan, "be sure to tell Him thank you for sending you a companion."

A chorus of yes'ums responded; then Jed and Nathan went up to the loft they shared, while Tom and Montgomery exited to the barn. Tom's room was actually the tack room of the barn, but it served him well, and a second cot was quickly set up for Montgomery. Soon all were fast asleep.

CHAPTER 4

Deputy Pettibone was a rather small man with an enormous mustache. His graying hair was thinning on top—an observation that could not be made of his upper lip. Wiry as a bottle brush and still golden in color, the mustache seemed to precede Pettibone into rooms as if it had a presence all its own.

He was proud of that mustache and proud of his hometown of Greenville as well. From Tommy Fitzgerald's fur trading post in 1845, Greenville had grown to a population of over five thousand in less than twenty years. It boasted not one but two churches, a school, four hotels and assorted smithies, livery stables, and saloons.

For all the commerce, though, there was only one general store. Occupying the most prominent site at the juncture of the road to Laver's Crossing and the stage route to the valley, Mullins' store represented civilization and its attendant comforts to the citizens of Greenville.

Replete with food items, cookstoves, yard goods, farm implements, the latest in weapons, and ammunition, Mullins supplied the needs of the community. Through him one could order seed from Iowa, a machine from Chicago to plant it, or a mahogany casket with real silver handles from far off New York for a person to be planted in.

Robert Mullins' boast was that he could arrange to have anything one could imagine delivered in only six short months.

Mullins the man was as expansive as the horizons his store boasted. Standing three inches shy of six feet, he nevertheless tipped the scales at three hundred pounds. The apparent absence of a neck seemed not to bother him at all; indeed, the compensation of having three chins seemed more than adequate. His hands, which were like lumps of bread dough, were never idle. He constantly fidgeted with his merchandise, especially the candy jars arrayed on a shelf behind his counter, or with his watch chain that stretched across his front like the trace-chain of a four-up team.

Deputy Pettibone, like others in these mountains, saw in Mullins a man of the world, knowledgeable and prosperous. As such his advice was often sought and his presence on school board and church council accepted as his natural due.

"And when I got the news, I came up from Tailholt pronto. Do you think we should get up a posse and get after Byrd?"

"Well now, Sheriff, you know that if Byrd has faded back into those hills, he'll be next to impossible to dig out. What's more, like it or not, it appears that the stranger made the first move. Even if you could locate Mr. Guidett and compel him to come in, he'd just get acquitted."

"But shouldn't we at least dig up that feller and hold an inquest?"

"Sheriff, you do as you think best, but unless you

intend to bring in the perpetrator, and I think we agree that's unreasonable, what's the point? The man is undeniably dead; he had no connections in this country, and apparently he deserved what he got—even your station-keeper Charlie admitted that, and he's the only witness."

"Well, not exactly. There was a small black child who saw it."

Mullins turned from the peppermint candy jar, which his sausage-like fingers had been exploring, and leaned across a case displaying bottles of Robin's Mild Cascara pills and Chicago Pharmaceutical's Diastalin tablets.

"A black child, you say? Did that dim-witted hostler know anything about the dead man other than that he came from Missouri?"

"Naw. He showed me a pitiful handful of stuff. 'Course Byrd had all his money. One strange thing: he had no letters, nor any papers telling who he was."

"You don't say? Well, perhaps he was a fugitive himself. Tell me, where is the child now?"

"Tom Dawson stopped there for the night. Byrd was for taking the black child away with him after the shooting, but Tom faced him down and then took the boy home."

"Did anyone think to see if the child had stolen anything?"

"No. No, least I don't think they checked. But here's Tom now; we can ask him."

Tom and Jesse entered Mullins' store and approached Deputy Pettibone.

"Hello, Jesse. Say, I was just fillin' Mr. Mullins in on what happened at Granite Station. "We—" Here he drew himself up to his full height and continued. "*We* think it's mighty peculiar that fella didn't have no name, nor any papers."

"The child he had along said the man's name was James—likely enough for a Missourian—and the boy had heard that name used for as long as he could remember."

"But was there no indication of the man's business?" This came from an attentive Mullins.

"No," Tom continued, "but there are many folk leaving that county who might not wish to bring any record of their past along."

"Quite, quite. And for a man who couldn't drink or gamble successfully, it's a wonder his lack of skill with guns wasn't discovered sooner also."

Deputy Pettibone felt the need to reassert his interrogation, so he asked, "Tom, are you certain that the child carried nothing away with him?"

Tom laughed. "No, Mike, that child barely had rags to cover himself. Fact is, he still thought he was a slave, and—say, there was one thing!" Tom slapped his pockets. "Yep, it's still here. When we went to bury that stranger, I must've slipped this in my pocket." Tom extracted the silver cuff link and laid it on the counter.

Before Deputy Pettibone could respond, Mullins' agitated fingers had grasped the jewelry and brought it close to his face. Just as quickly he laid it down again and commented, "It's nothing. Cheap workmanship. He probably lost the mate to it somewhere."

Jesse spoke up. "Didn't you say his name was James? Looks to me like this J is in the wrong spot. Who do you suppose J.D. could be, anyhow?"

"Ah, the man was a gambler, gentlemen. Most likely

he won *some* of the time. Perhaps this J.D., whoever he was, was even unlucky enough to lose his cuff link to the unfortunate Mr. James."

Pettibone scratched his head doubtfully and made as if to reach for the cuff link, but Mullins opened a drawer below the counter top and dropped it in.

"I'm sure it's nothing, but if I have time perhaps I can examine it further for a jeweler's mark—something to tell us of its origin."

Pettibone's mouth began to work, then shut with a snap, as did the drawer when Mullins threw his girth against it.

"Mike, Jesse and I want to talk to you about Byrd anyhow. Can we visit with you a bit?"

"Shore, Tom, come on to my place."

"No need to move, gentlemen," Mullins interjected. "Just pull up a couple of chairs here. Sheriff Pettibone was here seeking my advice about Guidett, so I'm sure he wouldn't mind if I listened to your opinions. Would you, Sheriff?"

Tom and Jesse looked at each other, but Deputy Pettibone had apparently made up his mind, and he started arranging three chairs and an empty crate of Weaver's soap flakes around the fireless potbelly cast iron stove.

Jesse began. "Mike, you know that stage hold up?"

"Yes, terrible thing. So coldblooded and all. The army's out lookin' into that right now, but I hear tell whoever did it covered their tracks right smart."

"Tom and I figure that Byrd and his partner could have done it, stashed the gold and then, by hard riding, made Granite in time to throw off the scent."

"Especially if they circled around to the northwest and came in over Shadow Ridge," Tom added.

"Gentlemen, gentlemen!" Mullins interrupted. "Byrd Guidett had neither the brains nor the ambition to challenge the army for a gold shipment. He's a poor desperado at best."

Pettibone addressed Tom. "Now, Tom, I came up from Tailholt by the only trail anywhere near Shadow Ridge, and comin' that way, they couldn't have made Granite by afternoon if they rode like the wind."

"I wan't thinking of the Tailholt trace, Mike. Jesse has heard talk of some older Indian trails—back in old Spanish days and even before. Why, even the old Yokut Chief Split Reed says that the mountain is haunted by the spirits of the Ancient Ones. Could be Byrd has found a lost trail across the south slope."

Robert Mullins' bulk obscured the ladder-back chair he occupied, but his words were anything but obscure. "Sheriff Pettibone, you know as well as I do that the south face of Shadow Ridge is a mass of deadfalls and brambles. Undoubtedly, the Indians regard it as haunted because any of their number who ventured there came to grief with a cliff or a rattlesnake. No, gentlemen, this is idle speculation. I certainly would not support endangering the lives of a posse of fine citizens for such a preposterous notion."

Tom's eyes flashed, but his brother laid a restraining hand on his arm and they both looked to the deputy for comment.

Pettibone's mustache worked vigorously as if chewing on what had been said. Finally he spoke, "Naw, boys, I'm glad you mentioned your idea but it won't wash. Like Mr. Mullins here says, there ain't no way around the south slope of old Shadow. Shucks, even pickin' his way along, Byrd would probably break his neck, let alone ridin' fast. Byrd's overdue for hangin', but this slaughter ain't his doin'."

Tom shook off Jesse's hand and stood up. "So that's it, huh? 'Thank you, Mr. Dawson, but *this* time Byrd didn't kill anybody worth bothering about?' Listen to me, Pettibone, if you ever want to be *sheriff*, as Mullins here keeps calling you, you'd better start thinking for yourself."

With that Tom and Jesse walked out, leaving a puzzled Deputy Pettibone and a complacent Mullins.

The store owner remarked, "The mark of a conscientious public servant is that he avoids irresponsible behavior. Bravo, Sheriff Pettibone, bravo."

The mustache puffed out proudly.

———

The dusty streets of Greenville were mostly deserted. The afternoon was hot and still. Tom's buckskin and Jesse's sorrel stood idly at the rail outside Mullins', their heads dropped and their eyes half closed. Even their tails were still, as though the oppressive heat had caused all the flies to seek shade.

"I guess that's that," Jesse commented. "You satisfied?"

"You know I'm not, but what else is there to do? What should we do with Mont?"

"He can stay, far as I'm concerned, but let's give him the choice. I'm sure Parson Swift could find a home for him, but he seems good-natured, and the boys are taken with him. Maybe he'll want to stay on."

"Before we head back, I want to get Matt to tighten that loose shoe—and maybe I can see what he thinks about old trails around Shadow Ridge."

"Good idea. If Tommy's at home, I can do the same with him. He knows most everything about this country as well as the Indians—better'n most."

Matt Green's blacksmith shop stood beneath a huge water oak just down the hill from Mullins' store. Green had taken the liberty of naming the town for himself, even though Tommy Fitzgerald had been the area's first white resident. Tommy had an Indian's outlook on land; he had never considered it something to be owned.

Matt was a wiry 60-year-old, as crusty and taciturn when sober as he was loudly abrasive when not. His face was framed by a gray beard that, together with his bushy eyebrows and craggy face, made him resemble Abraham Lincoln—until he opened his mouth. Matt seemed to have teeth only where they would meet the other jaw unopposed.

It was just as well that the likeness to Lincoln was not complete, because Matt was drunkenly outspoken in favor of the South. Not that he favored slavery, but he believed the southern states should be allowed to depart in peace.

Tom's friendly "howdy" produced no more than a grunt of response from Matt. The blacksmith was pulling on the wooden handle of a bellows suspended from the ceiling.

With each pull the glowing coals of his forge cast a shower of sparks upward. Matt's grizzled face was streaked with grime, as though scorched by the upward flight of the escaping cinders. The bar of iron barely visible amid the flames was already cherry red. With a last heave on the bellows handle, Matt grasped a pair of tongs with his left hand and pulled the iron from the fire, laying it across his anvil. A few deft strokes of his short-handled hammer bent it into a rough U-shape; then back into the fire it went. This process of alternately heating and hammering continued until with a convulsive last stroke, Matt thrust the now-recognizable mule shoe into the tempering bucket, producing an explosive blast of steam.

"Now, what can I do for ya, Dawson?" Matt's manner was gruff, but no more than usual for him.

"Buck's fixing to throw a shoe. I thought maybe you'd tighten it for me."

"Le's see, he was jest shod two weeks ago. Musta caught it on somethin'."

The two men walked out to where the buckskin stood, and Tom watched as Matt examined the right front hoof.

"Yup, I can clench it up some. Lemme finish this batch of mule shoes so's I can let the forge go out. It's too blasted hot for this work today."

"That's fine," Tom agreed. "Mind if I watch? I need to visit with you about something, anyway."

The blacksmith's eyes narrowed with suspicion. "What about?"

Tom began slowly. "Jesse and I have been talking about Shadow Ridge. In all the time I've been here, I never heard tell of any trail around the south slope."

" 'Cause there ain't none!" Even from one as crusty as Matt Green, the vehemence with which this was uttered was surprising.

"Why, surely there must be an old Indian trail or two—"

Matt's reply interrupted Tom's thoughts. "It's

48

naught but a death trap—pits and slide rock! Don't you be messin' thereabouts, see!"

"You don't believe it's haunted, do you?"

"Mebbe I do and mebbe I don't, but there can't nobody get round thataway, and that's all there's to it!"

Matt lapsed into a stony silence as he returned to work the bellows, leaving Tom to hope that his brother was having better success with the old mountain man, Tommy Fitzgerald.

"Light and set, boy, light and set." Tommy's reception of Jesse was as warm and genuine as he was old. It was said that even Tommy didn't know what his age was.

He had crossed the plains with Walker's expedition, surviving attacks by Shoshone and later Paiute war parties, and living through a near drowning. When he reached the high pass through the Sierras near a place now called Greenhorn, he stood amazed with the first group of Anglo explorers to see the great central valley of California.

Tommy had hunted Tule elk in the swamplands of the valley, but he always returned to this mountain home, located on, as he said, "the first level spot I set my foot on west of the mountains."

When the Mexican Alcaldes held sway over the southern California ranchos, when the Russian bear's presence was still felt in the North, and San Francisco was just a miserable Hudson's Bay outpost called "Yerba Buena," Tommy already had a thriving fur trading business.

Because of ample water and abundant acorns, the Yokuts had made their fall and spring home in these mountains. They were a nomadic people, moving their camp to the valley floor in winter and to the high mountains in summer. Tommy located his home at their crossroads, built an adobe cabin, and began to trade.

The Yokuts were not an aggressive people, and because game and fowl were so readily available, the tribe never lacked food. Nor did they feel any need of horses since they didn't depend on buffalo as their brothers of the Great Plains did. There had never been much cause for fighting, so they accepted Tommy's presence gratefully, as he gave them access to iron tools. They especially prized the white man's knives, having used only obsidian blades before.

The area, with its narrow, fast-flowing streams, was not suited for beaver, but the Yokuts traded in fox furs—both gray and red—and deer and elk hides.

Tommy had watched their numbers dwindle, mostly because of white man's diseases like cholera, until after forty years, very few remained. None came to trade with Tommy anymore, and now he sat outside the crude one-room adobe with his long white hair and beard, lost in his thoughts and occasionally taunted by Greenville school children.

At Tommy's invitation, Jesse dismounted and joined the old man in the shade of a gigantic water oak.

"How stands the Union, boy?"

This was Tommy's standard greeting and called for no particular acknowledgment, but today Jesse replied to the question.

"I guess it's on shaky ground these days, Tommy. From what I hear tell, it's taken some hard knocks lately."

"Ya don't say? But, boy, we can lick the Mex. For all

their trumpets, they can't match our long rifles, not by a long shot."

Jesse shook his head sadly. "No, Tommy, that Mexican war's been done these twenty years already. I mean this war between the states over slavery and all."

"Oh, I remember somethin' o' that now. I reckon I was back a ways there."

"That's all right, Tommy. I want you to remember back even further than that for me—back to old Injun days and before."

"What d'ya mean, boy?"

"Tommy, I know you know these hills like the back of your hand. Why, I bet you know every trail and blaze in them."

" 'Deed I do, boy, 'deed I do! Why, I come through here afore Fremont was a pup! I know'd Adams and Carson—all them folks. Why, I recollect one time Kit and me was—"

"Whoa up, Tommy," Jesse interrupted, for he saw that he had to jump in quickly before Tommy Fitzgerald had gotten completely wrapped up in his tale. "I want to hear you tell about these parts, especially the old trails around the south side of Shadow Ridge."

"Old Shadow? Why, boy, that mountain's haunted for sure. Plenty of good men lost their way, and ain't none of 'em come back—white nor Injun—neither."

"Think, Tommy, think. Weren't you ever on the south face?"

"Only oncet, boy, an' that were enough!"

Jesse leaned forward. "Tell me about that time."

Tommy closed his eyes for a moment as if collecting his thoughts; then with one hand gathering his beard and the other holding his forehead, he began.

"My pard, Matthews, him that's buried in Oak Grove next to the cedar stump, died up on ol' Shadow. One day he says to me, 'Tommy, I've shot a grizzly and let him get away. First light I'm goin' to track him round Shadow Ridge.'

"I says to him, 'Give it up, Frank; ya won't never find him.' And Matthews, he says, 'I cain't leave him go. If he lives he'll be rogue for sure.'

"So I said I'd go with him, and next morning we set out.

"Well, sir, we pushed round that south slope with the deer shrub and chaparral gettin' thicker an' thicker. We found a gob o' blood and we could foller that humpback real easy where he crashed through.

"When the track give up sudden-like, Matthews, he said to me, 'Be right canny now, Tommy; he's close.'

"An' jest as he said them words, all at once there riz up the biggest silver-tip I ever seed—right under his feet 'most like. Matthews tried to draw a bead, but that bear clubbed him jest as he shot. I believe Frank was dead afore he ever hit the ground.

"Well, sir, the bear never stopped to bother Matthews—jest come straight for me. I throw'd down on him and shot him in the eye—no further than from me to where you're sittin' now—but he never slowed down nor turned.

"I know'd I was a goner, but I drew my toothpick and run up the hill with that bear 'most on me.

"Do you know, I come on a path! Real faint—no more'n a trace, but goin' round the slope. I'm thinkin' maybe I'll distance this twice-shot bear when all at oncet I run plumb into a stone wall!

"I turned an' faced that there bear with jest my knife

and him agrowlin' an' snarlin' real fierce an' lookin' horrible with his one eye blowed all over his head. I was abackin' toward a clump of manzanita close by when it happened."

"What, Tommy? What happened?"

"I crashed into that manzanita, and next thing I was fallin'; and then crash, my head hit an' I didn't know no more.

"Well, sir, I come to with a cracked skull an' a busted elbow an' some busted-up ribs, but I was livin'. It was dark, so I laid real still to see if that grizzly was still nosin' about. I laid there clear to daybreak, hurtin' bad an' real scared.

"Come dawn I got the biggest scare yet, 'cause right over my head, leanin' down at me, was the grizz'! But he was stone dead! Yes, sir, he died right on the edge of that cave, an' me knocked out jest fifteen feet below him!"

"A *cave*, Tommy? You're sure it wasn't just a pit you'd fallen into?"

"Naw, boy, naw. When I came to myself I seed a stream of water an' a black hole arunnin' way back in the mountain. Some Indian signs, too, boy—paintin's on the rocks, real old an' all. I clumb up a rubble pile an' bless me if I didn't have to climb over that bear agettin' out!

"It took me 'most two days to get down out o' there, what with bein' busted up. I drug poor ol' Frank down to where we'd tied the horses, an' then I couldn't load him! I finally had to leave him an' ride for help. The Injuns brought him out an' buried him, an' they tended me through a ragin' fever.

"Well, sir, those Injuns said it was a good thing I'd

drug Frank as far as I did 'cause they wouldn't have set foot on the mountain proper. I said to myself, 'That's good enough for me. I ain't goin' back! An' I ain't never been back neither!"

"Didn't you ever tell this story to anyone else?"

"No, boy, I didn't. There wasn't nobody but the Injuns to tell it to at first; then later on I was afeared someone would get killed if they went lookin' for the cave, so I jest kept close till lately."

"Lately? You mean, just now?"

"Someone else asked me about a trail round ol' Shadow about a year ago. Said they'd heard Injuns talkin' about such. Well, I told 'em my story but cautioned 'em not to try an' find it—jest like I'm atellin' you now!"

"But who was it, Tommy? Who else asked about the trail?"

The old mountain man scratched his head for a moment and his eyes seemed momentarily glazed.

"What was that, boy? What did ya ask me?"

"I said, who else asked about Shadow Ridge?"

"I'm powerful sorry, boy, I can't remember. But say, did I ever tell ya about the grizzly I killed up on the Truckee? Say, that there was a bear! Why, boy, that bear was a' trackin' me!"

"Thank you, Tommy, but I'll have to hear that story another time," replied Jesse, standing up to go.

"Anytime, boy, anytime." The old man's head dropped, and he fell silent—but whether in sleep or deep thought, Jesse couldn't tell.

————

Riding back home, Jesse and Tom compared notes.

"I got nothin' from Matt at all—practically bit my head off for asking."

Jesse recounted Fitzgerald's story, bringing an exclamation from Tom.

"A trail *and* a cave—why, Jesse, that means that not only is there a way around, but maybe even a place to keep fresh mounts!"

"Ease up, Tom. Remember, Tommy's an old man and liable to get mixed up. I was excited, too, till I noticed that he likes to tell bear stories an awful lot and I remembered that he couldn't recall what year it is!"

"But at least we should go check it out, shouldn't we?"

"Well, I suppose so, but we needn't rush off tomorrow. We've got plenty to do around the place with those horses, and it's for certain that we'll get no one to go with us—not on the strength of old Tommy's recollections. Pettibone's mind is altogether made up for him by Mullins, so we'll be on our own.

"Anyway, they're probably right. How could a trail exist and no one even know about it? And even if there were such a path and Byrd could have used it, that doesn't prove that he did."

"There you go," snorted Tom, "just like you always did. You find out that something's possible but maybe a little chancey, and you start backin' up. How'd you ever get up your nerve to move out here, anyway?"

"I knew I had to be able to offer Em something mighty special to win her away from you, old son—it was worth the risk. Now just let be till we get all our projects caught up; then I'll go with you if you still think it's so all-fired important."

CHAPTER 5

The cabin showed no signs of having been lived in for years. Its squared timber had once been mortared, but the chinking had been allowed to fall into such disrepair that more spaces than mortar appeared.

The windows were gaping holes only partially covered by ragged flaps of cowhide, and the wood-plank door hung crookedly from a torn leather hinge. Set in a side canyon through which flowed a seasonal tributary of Cedar Creek, the site was the graveyard of some long-gone miner's hopes for wealth.

Mullins stopped to lean against a gnarled buckeye that stood just at the edge of the cabin's clearing. Panting for breath after his hike up the canyon from where he had left his rig hidden just off the main road to Greenville, he peered through the clumps of elderberry bushes and mopped his face.

Inwardly he swore and muttered to himself at the apparent emptiness of the scene; then he heaved his bulk forward a few more steps. He stopped short at a movement in the doorway and peered through squinted, piglike eyes as Byrd Guidett strolled out.

"I know'd it was you. I heerd ya wheezin' and crashin' through the brush a mile off."

"Shut up, you fool, and get back inside!" snarled Mullins "Where's Yancey?"

"Here." A voice at Mullins' elbow made him jump and caused even more sweat to pour down his florid face. Yancey stepped out from behind a brush-obscured boulder, replacing a gleaming knife into his boot top as he did so.

The three moved into the cabin. Yancey and Byrd stood on either side of the crumbling stone fireplace. On the oak beam mantel lay Byrd's rifle. The room was otherwise bare except for a rough bench on which Mullins seated himself.

"We done it!" boasted Byrd. "The strong box is hid and no one left to mark us for the law! We come over slick as ya please and made as though we hadn't a care except to play some cards. 'Course, we had a little set-to at Granite, but we came off none the worse for it."

Mullins exploded. "You cussed fool! None the worse? Do you know who it was you killed? That Missourian was Colonel James. He'd been working undercover since the secession. He was here to deliver my commission from President Davis personally and to take charge of raising the Army of the Pacific!"

"What? That ol' drunk a colonel?"

Yancey spoke up, his gray face more animated that one would have thought possible. "He didn't give no recognition sign. How was we supposed to know?"

Mullins turned on him, his jowls quivering with rage. "Did you expect him to announce himself to any cutthroat brigand he came across? He was on his way to meet with me. The gold you stole was to be used to purchase arms and train our fighting force to lead California out of the Union! *He* had the names of our contacts for making the purchases!"

"But, boss," said Byrd, "we got the gold. Cain't we jest buy the guns ourselves?"

"Do you think we can go to any arms dealer in San Francisco and say, 'Please, sir, we'd like to buy three hundred rifles'?" We'd be in Fort Alcatraz before you could cry 'Pinkerton' and hanged shortly after!"

A somewhat subdued Byrd lapsed into silence, and after a moment Yancey asked, "What's to be done?"

"The talk is that James had no papers on him—in fact, nothing but the cuff link, which I very fortunately got into my possession before anyone asked too many questions. That must mean that he had hidden the papers somewhere until after he made contact with me. Perhaps he felt that he was being followed or might be searched."

"But, boss, there's ten miles of boulders around Granite station! How'll we ever find 'em?"

Mullins calmed down a little and looked thoughtful. "Maybe that nigger boy can show us where they stopped before Granite. Or maybe Colonel James even gave the papers to the boy to carry."

"I know'd I should've catched that nigger! See, Yancey, I told ya we shoulda had him!"

Yancey replied dryly, "I seem to recall you not wantin' to press the issue with Tom Dawson and Mr. Colt's child."

Byrd glared at Yancey, but Mullins silenced any reply by saying, "Enough of this! Colonel James's death was an unfortunate accident, which luckily for you, Byrd Guidett, is reported to be not entirely your fault."

"Not entirely my fault! Why, he—"

"Shut up, I tell you! Now listen; it's clear what must

be done. We must eliminate any curiosity about Shadow Ridge. There must be no snooping anywhere near the quartz ledge. Secondly, we must have that child!"

Tom and Jesse had chosen a half dozen of the stoutest old oak trees around the place to tie the broncos to. Saddled and cinched, the first six horses in the string were tied high and tight to the strongest limb of a tree. Cotton rope hobbled their legs and another rope wound around the rib cage and up through the forelegs, then through the halter to create a harness that would squeeze hard whenever the animal fought to pull away from the tree where it had been tied.

A critter what won't stand polite at a hitchin' rail is gonna come over backwards an' kill hisself an' maybe somebody else! That had been the first rule Tom and Jesse had learned from their Missouri horse-trader father. In the years since, the brothers had seen enough spoiled horses fighting a hitching rail to know the fact for themselves.

Even though there were a hundred ways to break a mustang, the brothers started by letting each animal teach itself a few manners. Some fought the rope and the tree branch more than others, jumping back and straining until they almost sat down on their hind legs, then lunging forward to relieve the pressure of the taut rope around their girth. Other horses learned to stand still after only one or two halfhearted battles. One thing was certain: they all learned sooner or later that it was easier to stand politely, regardless of the commotion around them, than to fight the rope.

It was the job of Jed, Nathan, and Montgomery—

Mont as he soon came to be called—to wave flour sacks and holler like Indians within the view of the tied horses, but safely out of range of flying hoofs and the thrashing of bodies of a thousand pounds of unhappy horseflesh. *Sacking the horse* was the term Tom gave this process. After a while, the horses stopped quivering and totally ignored the bellowing of the small ranch hands.

Seven of the more stubborn animals fought for days. One powerful young bay stood sweating beneath the saddle for nearly a week, receiving from the hand of his tormentors food and a bucket of water twice a day until, at last, the brawny animal nickered happily at the sight of the man who had trussed him up like a prisoner. Tom chose this horse for his own. He had spirit and a will, and once Tom had tamed the spirit and turned the will into a desire to please, the big bay had the promise of being a fine mount.

Except for his strength and size, the animal was anything but handsome. His large head had a curve like a Roman nose. The lower lip protruded slightly and moved incessantly as though he were trying to speak. His legs were black and blended into four iron-hard black hoofs. The black hoofs were an attribute that pleased Tom. An animal with white stockings meant soft, white feet, which were less likely to hold up in the harsh mountain terrain.

"This fella will go from here to the Atlantic and never need to be shod," Tom commented as he picked up the foot and examined it. "Let them have their pretty horses. I'll take good legs any day."

Emily overheard Tom's proud mumbling as she walked by with a basket of laundry in her arms. "Well, he is anything *but* pretty," she laughed. "It is lucky for us that the Union Cavalry is buying these creatures by the head. They certainly have the biggest heads of any horses I have ever seen!"

"I'm keeping this fella." Tom hefted a heavy sack of feed onto the saddle of the still-tied animal. "Jugheaded though he is."

Emily nodded. "Then name him Duncan!" she said, not missing a beat. "As a personal favor to me." She smiled brightly.

"Duncan?" Tom scratched his head. "Why Duncan?"

She continued back to the house with her basket, still giggling at her secret joke. *"Duncan!"* she called over her shoulder.

Tom shrugged and patted the thick neck of the bay. "I christen thee Duncan," he said. "Whoever he was, he must have been ugly as a mongrel dog!"

As if in agreement, the newly named Duncan nickered.

———

Jed, Nathan, and Mont were ready for school the morning the first twenty of the army's horses were gathered for delivery to Fort Tejon.

Tom mounted his big bay horse and then hefted Mont up for a proud ride around the barn. Duncan had learned quickly and pliantly when Tom had begun to ride him in the round pen. Now, while the rest of the rough string of mustangs were still reining reluctantly, Duncan moved easily to the leg pressure of his rider.

Emily had packed more than enough for the four-day journey. She kissed Jesse goodbye and then stepped back as he swung the pack over the saddle and mounted.

"Be careful, won't you?" She looked worried for a moment, then added, "He will give His angels charge over thee, to keep thee in all thy ways!"

Jesse sounded a gruff *amen* in response, then leaned down to kiss her farewell once again. Tom looked away at their embrace. It was obvious that Jesse did not want to leave Emily for even a short journey.

Tom issued a spate of orders to the boys. Feeding and milking and other chores would have to continue even with the men gone. A chorus of eager assurance came from Jed and Nathan and Mont, who now seemed to fit into the family as easily as the others.

Tom was surprised when Emily reached up and briefly took his hand in her own. "Look after my Jesse, now," she whispered.

Tom cleared his throat and pushed his hat back on his head. "He's always been the one looking after me; you know that." Something in her eyes made him uncomfortable. He looked away, staring between the ears of the big bay horse. "When are you going to tell me why I'm calling this horse Duncan, anyway?" he asked. "Here I am taking him to a fort full of Union soldiers; Lord knows this horse is ugly enough to draw fire. Someone is gonna ask me, Emily, why I've named this jughead *Duncan*!"

"Tell us, Emily!" Jesse urged jokingly. "Just think, if we were ambushed by Indians you'd have to live with the fact that we never knew."

Her eyes flashed anger. "No such talk now, Jesse Dawson!" she scolded. "But if you must know, I've named him for an old black preacher who had a lower lip just like that! And whenever he was asked to pray, he'd tug his lip and say, 'De Lawd *done can* do it, suh!

Ah knows de Lawd *done can!*"

There was a terribly awkward moment when Mont looked startled at her rendition of the black preacher's dialect. He blinked and then looked at the horse and said loudly, "Well, I'd say de Lawd *done can* do 'bout anything He want to! He done he'ped get dem hosses broke, and now He *done can* bring Mistuh Jesse an' Mistuh Tom home safe-like!"

There was a burst of laughter all around, and then Mont patted the muscled shoulder of the horse. "Duncan!" he said with finality, and with a whistle, Jesse and Tom began to move the herd down the lane.

"Hee-yah!" shouted Jesse.

"Whoop! Whoop!" urged Tom as the last of the string of twenty green-broke mustangs were turned into the stock pens at Fort Tejon.

The steps of the adobe buildings were lined with spectators, civilians and off-duty soldiers alike. The drive from the range in Linn's Valley had taken four days, but now it was successfully concluded. The cavalry captain who gestured for the gate to be closed behind the last horse nodded with satisfaction at the sight.

"They look fine, gentlemen, just fine," he called to Tom and Jesse, who sat their horses flanking the gate. "Who would have thought that you could take wild and scrawny horseflesh and turn it into such sleek appearance in such a short span of time?"

"Well, Captain," commented Jesse, "all we did was catch this bunch at a watering hole up Mojave way inside a box canyon. We drifted out the ones we didn't want, and then we kept the others fenced away from water for a few days, only givin' them to eat and drink by our own hand. After about a week they got mostly docile."

Here Tom took up the tale. "Well, sir, next we got a rope on that lead mare over yonder." He pointed out a tall bay horse with a white blaze on her face that ran up into one blue eye. "When we started for home, she led real easy, and the rest of the herd just followed along."

Jesse resumed describing the route back to the ranch by explaining how they had gone over Walker Pass, forded the Kern River, and then followed the Bull road across the Sierra to home.

"After crossing the river, these horses were in feed like they'd never seen out in the desert. They didn't have any more reason to run away, and with this mare leading the way, the rest came on pretty easy."

"As for sleek," Tom pointed out, "all they needed was a few weeks of good feed. When we were culling the herd, we took care to pick only the sound ones that showed their ancestry back to the granddaddy horses brought to this country by the Spanish folk. Blood will tell, given time and opportunity, and this bunch has shaped up real well."

"Of course, gentlemen, how well they shape up as cavalry mounts remains to be seen," pointed out the captain. "Well fed they may be and able to be driven, but green broke to the colonel's satisfaction is another matter."

"I thought you might be interested in that, Captain," remarked Tom. "So I'd like you to look at Duncan here."

"I can already tell that you didn't select this animal for his beauty, Mr. Dawson. Perhaps you should tell me why I'm to pay attention to him."

"You see, Captain, Duncan here came out of that same herd at the same time as the rest. Now, he's had a little extra work put on him by me special, but nothing your boys couldn't do with their mounts. Watch this."

Tom spun Duncan around on his hind legs and galloped off toward the large oak tree under which explorer Peter Lebec had been killed by a grizzly. Duncan flashed around it, turning so close as to enable Tom to reach upward in passing and grasp a handful of leaves from a low branch. Halfway back across the parade ground, Tom jerked the horse to a sudden stop, and Duncan almost skidded as he sat back on his haunches.

Tom next worked the horse in a tight series of circles and figure eights, then trotted him back over to the watching crowd. Drawing rein before the grinning captain, Tom slid from Duncan's back to stand beside the bay as if to say, *See, nothing to it at all.*

"Excellent! Just excellent. And you say the rest of the string can come as far in as little time?"

"There's no doubt about it, Captain. After all, this one is not only jugheaded to look at; he's the most pigheaded and stubborn one of the bunch."

"And you say you can have the remaining twenty here in short order?"

"Absolutely," promised Jesse. "And there's more where these came from too."

"Well, then, get them to us just as quickly as possible, and perhaps we'll be doing business in a regular way. Why don't we go into my office and see about your payment?"

"Suits us," said Jesse with a smile. "Then we'll be startin' back to get to work on the next batch."

As they walked up the steps, a portly quartermaster

sergeant called out to Tom, "Hey, Dawson, this here crop's livelier than potatoes, huh?" To the roar of laughter which erupted, Tom waved good-naturedly and replied, "Yes, and you'd best be careful, Sergeant. Fork one of these spuds wrong, and you'll be the one gettin' peeled!"

The young lieutenant leading the detail of four troopers was preparing to leave at the same time as the Dawson brothers, so they all rode together as far as the crossing of Cottonwood Creek.

"We'll be turning west there toward the ranch of Colonel Thomas Baker," he remarked, raising his eyebrows significantly.

When neither brother reacted to this announcement, he continued, "Baker is being arrested for interfering with recruiting efforts for the Union army. He has been very open about his pro-rebel sentiments, but has recently gone too far."

"Isn't Baker some kind of government man himself?" inquired Tom.

"Yes, he's a state senator, and he's been using his political opportunities to ridicule the Union army and describe in detail the defeats we have experienced at rebel hands. He's even gone so far as to say that the war is no concern of Californians, and that boys from here ought not go off to fight in it. He stops just short of treason by pretending to favor a peaceful settlement to the conflict, but we believe that he privately favors pulling California out of the Union.

"Anyway," he concluded, "he's to be arrested on the recruiting charge, and that should interrupt his little schemes for a while."

CHAPTER 6

Byrd crouched behind a cottonwood tree that grew up from the creek bed. He was peering through its leaves toward the mouth of the canyon out of which the stage would have to emerge. Dust devils chased each other across the intervening plain. Byrd scrutinized each one to see if it would resolve itself into the coach and four that he was expecting, but for over an hour each round wind had been a false alarm.

He was annoyed that the coach was late. The dust from the dry creek bed caught at his throat and irritated his eyes. For a time he amused himself by plucking cottonwood leaves and dropping them one by one at his feet, but he soon grew tired of this and drew a stained bandanna from around his neck and mopped his forehead.

He turned the bandanna over briefly in his hands, considering whether to tie it around his face. He glanced again toward the stage road, squinted upward at the sun, and threw the bandanna down on the ground in disgust.

Nervous at this delay, he decided to check his Walker Colt to make sure it was loaded properly. He reached for the four-pound pistol he wore tied down and drew its nine-inch length carefully from the holster and regarded it with squinted eyes.

Someone had once remarked that the only thing Byrd cared about in all the world besides himself was the six-shooter. Byrd would never have thought to express that observation in just that way, but it was nevertheless true, and with good reason. He earned his livelihood by his ability with the Walker's faithful performance, and it had saved his life on more than one occasion. Of course, it had not been able to save the Texas Ranger from whom Byrd had obtained it.

The weapon was loaded and capped as it had been the two earlier times Byrd had checked, and he swore at himself for this apparent nervousness. He was, he decided, tired of waiting. Being tired made him grouchy, like a petulant child in need of a nap.

He had just returned the Colt to its holster when he heard Yancey's signal—a low, whistled quail call that sounded like "chicago, chicago." Byrd's head snapped up, the revolver again in his hand.

Yancey would nag him later for not spotting the coach first. This thought only served to increase his irritation. Sure enough, out from the canyon a moving black shape had appeared, throwing up a trail of dust behind.

On through the sagebrush it came, presently drawing near enough for the form of the coach to be seen. A little closer, and the team of mules drawing it could be made out; shortly after, Byrd could see the driver and a shotgun messenger perched on the box.

Any nervousness Byrd might have felt vanished. Now he was all business. He stooped over and retrieved the bandanna, but his eyes never left the approaching stage. With his left hand he drew the cloth around his neck and swore again at the awkwardness of trying to knot it one-handed. He replaced the .44 momentarily, just long enough to tie the kerchief and pull its folds up over his nose. His bushy red beard pushed the mask out from his face.

He looked down the draw to where Yancey squatted, similarly masked and armed. Byrd had a moment to sneer again at Yancey's choice of weapons. It was a .36 caliber Allen, a "pepperbox"—good for a hideout weapon, but not a man's gun, in Byrd's opinion.

His attention returned to the stage, now less than four hundred yards away. Their plan was simple. Since the seldom-wet creek bed had no bridge, the stage drivers were in the habit of pitching violently down one bank and back up the other without even slackening speed. Just below the rim of the bank nearest the stage, Byrd and Yancey had laid the trunk of a cottonwood. This unexpected obstacle should cause the lead mules to balk, and in the confusion Byrd and Yancey would have the opportunity to get the drop on the driver and guard.

Byrd could see the pair of men clearly now. The driver was leaning forward, skillfully working the lines, getting the utmost speed out of the surging team. The guard was leaning back, bracing himself against the expected swoop into the gully. Sunlight glinted dully on the barrels of the shotgun he carried.

As expected, the coach didn't even slow as it passed the crest of the creek bank. Over it came, the team dipping below the rim so rapidly that the wagon appeared to be propelled straight across the wash for a space before dropping to follow the contour. Right in front of the leaders was the tree, its branches right in their startled faces.

The driver didn't even have time to react and had

no chance to halt the suddenly pitching team; for as the leaders attempted to swerve, the sudden loss of rhythm caught the wheelers off guard, slewing the coach violently to the left, then turning it over on its side with a rending crash. The driver flew off the box after the team, and the guard pitched over the tree trunk in the direction of the tumbling coach, which finally came to rest on its side, surrounded by a great cloud of dust.

As the dust began to clear low moans could be heard coming from the coach's interior. One wheel made a mournful creaking sound as it continued to revolve lazily on its now vertical axle.

Byrd straightened up and pushed his hat up off his forehead in astonishment. He glanced to where Yancey also was taking in the scene of wreckage with an amazed look on his face. They had expected to stop the stage's headlong rush, but nothing like this.

Anticipating no resistance from the destruction that presented itself, both men put away their weapons, Yancey thrusting the pepperbox into his waistband.

They converged on the coach from opposite sides. Byrd wore a whimsical grin as if he wished he could always conduct a robbery in such a spectacular manner.

Yancey, normally silent, was moved to what was for him garrulous speech. "Did ya see that, Byrd? I'll be a suck-aig mule if that weren't the most horrific crash. Them fellers didn't have no chance atall."

Byrd studied the scene with a proprietary air, noting with satisfaction that the guard's neck was bent at an impossible angle; he was dead. Then Byrd spoke. "Where'd that driver get off to? Last I seen, he was sailin' after them mules. Well, no matter, he musta fetched up in the next county in so many little pieces, they'll have to pick 'em up with a dustpan and a broom."

That the occupants of the coach still lived was evidenced by their occasional groaning. Even though there appeared to be little chance of fight left in anyone who had experienced the crash, Yancey pulled his pistol again before stepping up on the useless thoroughbrace and peering down into the interior.

"Thar's only one in here, and he looks busted up bad," called Yancey.

"Leave 'em then, and let's get to business."

The two undid the boot and found the expected strong box. It had not broken open in the crash, but the hinges were bent, and Byrd soon was able to pry the hasp and lock off the case.

Inside was a shelf of official-looking documents, which Byrd thrust into his shirt unread. As a matter of fact, he couldn't have read them, anyway. Beneath the papers was the gold—about ten thousand dollars' worth.

Byrd hefted the box to his shoulder and turned to slog through the sand to where they had tethered the horses. Yancey trudged alongside.

An arresting pair of clicks brought them to a sudden halt. Beside the body of the guard stood the driver. His bloodless face was drawn with pain, and his left arm dangled limp at his side.

But Byrd's attention was centered on the man's right side, where he cradled the guard's shotgun under the crook of his arm and had just thumbed back the hammers.

In a halting voice he ordered, "Throw down that box and your weapons." Byrd and Yancey complied, each fingering their pistols gently in the face of the double-barreled threat.

"Now raise your hands and keep 'em up." With a glance at each other, Byrd and Yancey did so, while moving slightly apart. The driver's strength was failing; he had difficulty keeping the shotgun's muzzle elevated.

"Listen, mister, yer stove up bad, and so's yer passenger. Now ya'd best let us ride outta here, an' we'll send back some help."

"Shut up, you two, I need to think," mumbled the driver.

"But yer man here, he needs help now—cain't ya hear 'im?

As if on cue a frightened moan came from the coach. In the instant that the driver's attention wavered, Yancey's hand flashed downward toward his shirt collar and upward again with the knife that had hung between his shoulders.

The shotgun discharged both barrels into the ground with a roar, but the blade that now quivered in the man's stomach occupied all his attention.

Byrd scooped up his .44, but it wasn't needed. A moment of startled disbelief crossed the driver's face, and he swayed forward once, then pitched face-first into the sand.

Byrd and Yancey rode off, laughing at how easy it had been.

———

Seven men rode downward out of the narrow pass guarded by Fort Tejon, through a rocky sagebrush-covered ravine, and out onto the gentler slope that led to the floor of the San Joaquin Valley.

The dusty haze of Indian summer obscured their view up the valley, but even so it was a magnificent sight.

Stretching some three hundred miles from where they rode to the San Francisco Bay and beyond, the great central valley was crisscrossed with waterways, swamps and marshes. Here and there herds of Tule elk roamed.

As they rode, Tom caught more than one of the troopers casting admiring looks at Duncan. Homely he might be, but they could tell at a glance that he had heart. These hardened men knew the value of a reliable horse. Patrolling the reaches of the Great Desert as they did, there had to exist implicit trust between man and beast. In the previous year's campaign against the Mojave Indians, the lieutenant himself had been saved from an agonizing death by his mount's ability to locate water when the tank they were depending on had turned out unexpectedly empty.

So when Duncan snorted and pricked his ears forward, not only Tom but Jesse and the whole party took note. They were just approaching the intersection of their northward-bound track and the road that led westward from the mines. The breeze was blowing toward them, and suddenly all their animals gave evidence of uneasiness.

The lieutenant called a halt and stood in his stirrups, craning his neck and peering forward. "I see something in the bend of the creek yonder," he stated. "Jones, you and Brown go forward and reconnoiter."

"Aye, sir," the troopers responded, and galloped forward. A few moments later one of them returned at high speed.

"All right, Trooper Brown, report."

An ashen-faced Brown burst out, "They're all dead, sir! I mean, it's the stage, sir, and it's been wrecked!"

"An accident, Trooper?"

"Yes, sir . . . I mean, no sir—that is, we thought it was, sir, with the coach all busted up. The guard, sir, he's got a busted neck. And the passenger, he's dead too."

"Well, what makes you think it isn't an accident?"

"It's the driver, sir, he—"

"Speak up, Brown, what is it?"

"The driver, sir, he's got six inches of knife stuck in him!"

An investigation of the area revealed in short order how the holdup had been accomplished. They could see where the outlaws had waited to surprise the stage and how successful they had been. From the position of the driver's body and the discharged shotgun lying beside it, it was even possible to reconstruct how he had met his fate.

"How could this happen?" began Jesse. "After that other holdup with everyone murdered, why wasn't this stage escorted?"

"Great scott, man!" returned the lieutenant testily. "Don't you know how short-handed we're running here? This patrol is half its normal strength, and on top of that, has twice its usual assignment to patrol!"

"Look, Lieutenant," Jesse replied, "we know you've got your problems, but this can't be allowed to continue. Pretty soon no one will feel safe traveling through the valley. Already folks are starting to talk about the need to form a California militia to mount our own patrols. People are saying that if the army can't or won't protect us, then we'll have to do it ourselves."

"May I warn you, Mr. Dawson, that kind of talk is precisely what the so-called *Colonel* Baker is being arrested for!"

"Listen," broke in Tom, "we're not talking politics

here; we're talking the safety of our families. Whether this is some rebel plot or plain old highway robbery makes precious little difference to folks who lose their lives or their loved ones!"

The lieutenant looked subdued for a moment before he spoke. "Of course you're right, and the ones who did this and the other holdup must be brought to justice as quickly as possible. We still believe that this is all linked up with the plot to introduce rebel elements into the control of California gold. There may even be a bigger conspiracy afoot than you or I can imagine."

"I know," added Jesse, "that there are those in the mountains who have no use for the government in Washington; they just want to be left alone. But that doesn't necessarily make them favor the Southern cause, nor get them involved in robbery and murder!"

"I'm aware of that, Mr. Dawson, but you can certainly see we need help if this situation is to be remedied. Suppose we were to make an appearance in Greenville and other communities, pledging our increased attention to the problem, while at the same time requesting the cooperation of all the citizens in locating those who have done this?"

Jesse turned to Tom. "What do you think, Tom? Would that help matters any?"

"I don't know, Jesse. It's certain that once the news of this holdup gets out, there's going to be a real uproar. I'm not trying to tell the army its business, but it seems to me that if they'd admit we've got a problem and work together with us to solve the situation, it would be the right approach."

Tom continued to address the officer. "Don't expect any of the mountain folk to come up with information about rebel sympathizers among their friends and neighbors. They won't tolerate thieves and murderers, but they believe a man's politics are his own business— at least as far as his thoughts are concerned."

"Very well, gentlemen, I'll communicate your views to my commanding officer. I feel certain he'll agree that some immediate action will be required. Meanwhile, if you see the local deputy—what's his name, the one with the enormous mustache?"

"Pettibone?"

"That's the one. Would you inform him about what's happened and ask him to communicate it to the sheriff and others? We'll try to pass along any helpful information just as soon as we can."

———

The scene of the wrecked stagecoach and murdered men was still vivid in the minds of Tom and Jesse as they rode the final mile into Greenville. Neither had spoken for hours. Anger at the first sight of such a violent crime had finally dissipated into helpless frustration. Whoever had done this thing was long gone—vanished without leaving so much as a single track on the stony paths that led from the scene. Tom and Jesse would inform Deputy Pettibone that once again the gold destined for the Union coffers had been stolen. But there was little that could be done, and hardly an ounce of sentiment would be spared for the stolen Yankee gold. Wasn't there a war on, after all? Didn't people get hurt in wars, even here in California?

Tom had seen this sort of thing a hundred times in Missouri. Senseless killing. Murder in the name of a cause. Somehow people here needed to understand that there was something else at issue. Something more cruel than war. What was it? He had tried to figure it out before. How could he put a name to the cold chill that had coursed through him at the grisly sight he had seen?

As if reading his thoughts, Jesse turned to him. "Whoever did that enjoyed killing. There was an evil love of death."

Tom did not need to reply. Yes. That was it. That was what he had seen on the Kansas-Missouri border. He had even glimpsed that evil in his own soul. Now, as if to escape the landslide of emotions and memories which engulfed him, he spurred Duncan into a gentle lope up the last hill before reaching town.

At the top of the rise, a new sound greeted him. A cloud of dust rose up from the schoolyard. Boys shouted and little girls shrieked as two dozen children pressed in for a better view of a miniature battle.

"Get 'im!"

"Whallop that nigger, Sam!"

"Hit 'im . . . in the face!"

"Kill them Yankee lovers!"

Tom rose up slightly in his stirrups and tapped Duncan, who raced toward the schoolyard.

So it had come here as well. Even among the children, who mimicked their parents. . . .

CHAPTER 7

"Raw pieces of beef steak. Just the thing for black eyes." Jesse handed out the evening's uncooked supper to each of the three boys. "Just hold it there over your shiner. I reckon it will still make a good meal after you're done using it." Jesse winked at Emily in an effort to lighten her mood. She had not smiled since her first look at the dusty, battered boys.

Mont bit his lip and peered up at Jesse through swollen eyes. He had taken the worst beating, and now Jesse wondered how the child could see. "Um, Mistuh Jesse . . ." He looked at the meat in his hand and held it timidly as though he was afraid to put it to his bruised eye.

"Yes. What is it, Mont?" Jesse knelt and put his hands on the boy's shoulders. He was keenly aware what young Mont must be feeling. After all, hadn't the fight been over the color of his skin? That and the sale of horses to the Yankees?

"Well, suh . . ." He continued to gaze at the meat. "Should ah be puttin' dis here meat on my eyes, too?"

"Of course, Mont!" Emily chimed in, wanting to reassure Mont that he was as much a part of the family as Jed and Nathan. "It's only a bit of beefsteak, and there's plenty more where that came from. You must not worry about that!"

"Yessum. Ah mean . . . no, ma'am." He still looked uneasy. "What ah means is . . . if'n dis is gonna take away my black eyes . . . is it . . . I mean, it ain't gonna make white round my eyes . . ." His small voice trailed off. "Is it? It'd be plumb awful if I was to go back to school all spotted like!"

Suppressing a laugh, Jesse reassured him that the beefsteak would simply take away the welts. Emily guided Mont's hand up to his swollen face and then sat him down firmly at the kitchen table next to Jed and Nathan.

With a solemn shake of her head, she led Jesse to the door and stepped out onto the porch.

"What next?" She wrung her hands distractedly.

Jesse lifted her chin gently and looked into her eyes. "How about a kiss hello?" he asked, pulling her close and brushing her lips with his.

"Oh, Jesse!" She leaned heavily against her husband. "I'm so worried. We had so hoped to be spared from this terrible war. But even *here* . . . people are so—" She did not finish. Jesse was stroking her hair as if she were a child to be comforted.

"It was only a kid's schoolyard fight. Nothing to fret over."

"No." She began to weep softly. "It's more than that. Not just Mont. Children can be so cruel! But . . . Jess, Mrs. Burton had harsh words for me at church, and—"

"Mrs. Burton? At church, no less. Emily you can't—"

"Listen to me, Jesse!" Emily stepped back and held the face of her husband in her hands. "I'm *frightened!* People don't take kindly to you and Tom breaking horses for the army. When I got home from church yesterday, someone had opened a gate! Five horses were turned loose! Five of the best. I thought it was just a malicious prank at first, but then I got to thinking about what Mrs. Burton said about how *many* folks are angry about those horses! I could scarcely sleep last night for thinking about it. And now, today, the boys get into it. And not only that, you come back with word that there's been another robbery—men killed and Union gold stolen . . ." She looked fiercely away at the setting sun. "I thought we would be free from this sort of thing here in California. The Promised Land. Free from war and killing and prejudice."

Jesse sighed and leaned against the porch railing as he followed her gaze to Shadow Ridge. "It wouldn't matter where we lived, Emily," he said softly as weariness crept into his voice. "You know that. Folks are always finding some reason to make trouble, to stir things up. You know it's not just the war between Yankees and rebels that has people riled up." He put his arm around her. "It's a different war. The war is inside men's hearts. Fierce and mean. And I don't suppose it's any different anywhere. No better or worse. Folks just love to hate."

The sky darkened and the trill of crickets filled the cool evening air. Neither Emily nor Jesse spoke for a long time. At last, when the corralled horses nickered for their supper, Emily said quietly, "The boys and I managed to round up three of those jugheaded horses of yours. Two are still out there wandering around Shadow Ridge, I suppose."

"Be careful how you speak of those jugheads. They are money in the bank—pure gold beneath those scruffy hides. Tom and I will go find those two."

"Jesse!" She began to protest, but he had already gone to find Tom.

Colonel Mason was trying his best to keep his temper under control. He knew if he responded emotionally to what he was hearing, he would lose the attention of the meeting. It wasn't easy, though, given what Matt Green had been saying.

"Yer bunch of blue-bellied scoundrels couldn't track a black bear on a snow-covered hillside! You ain't up here to try and catch no robbers; ye're jest makin' up stories so's to get folks to rat on their neighbors!"

"Now that's not all true, Mr. Green; we have reason—"

"I'll give you reason! I'll give you reason! You can't catch no holdup men no more'n all the Yankee gen'rls that was ever spawned can catch the likes of Jubal Early or Robert E. Lee! You ain't showed nothin' to me, 'cept that now you got an excuse to go off achasin' poor folks what don't want to fight no Yankee war!"

There were muttered growls of approval at these sentiments.

"If I may be allowed to respond—"

"Here's my ree-spond!" Matt made as if to spit, but caught himself just in time. "Sorry, Parson, I disremembered where we was."

"Thank you for recollecting that this is a church, Mr. Green. Now perhaps we should allow the colonel to continue."

Matt subsided, muttering to himself.

"Thank you, Parson Swift. Here is the situation from the army's point of view. Gold belonging to the United

States government has been stolen. That makes the affair our concern. Civilians have been killed in those same attacks. That makes it a case for the civilian authorities as well. Now, whether or not you believe that the robberies are politically motivated, the fact remains that such attacks cannot be allowed to continue.

"As much as it pains me to admit it, thus far Mr. Green is correct. All our efforts to date have not apprehended the culprits, which is what brings us to the point of today's meeting.

"Contrary to what Mr. Green thinks, we are not here to pursue draft-dodgers or deserters, or to inquire into anyone's personal beliefs." Here Colonel Mason paused briefly to look Matt Green squarely in the eye before continuing. "It is necessary for us to pursue whatever information we possess, and that information is that these robberies are linked to a conspiracy to promote the rebel cause.

"Now, we are prepared to see that every stage has an armed escort and to mount regular patrols of the highways in order to prevent further occurrences. What we want from you good people is a report of any suspicious activities, any strangers in town, or known outlaws whose movements seem questionable."

Matt Green burst out with another interruption. "There, ya see what I'm atellin' ya? Who's an outlaw far's the army is concerned? What's sur-spicious?"

He seemed disposed to continue his tirade, but at the front corner of the room Robert Mullins rose to his feet, graciously smiling. "With all due respect, Mr. Green, I think that the colonel has made it very clear that it is up to us as good citizens to determine what is reported and what is not. It will be on each of our consciences to come forward with information that might prove helpful. After all, we want the army to participate in defending the citizenry from this wanton depredation until such time as our own capable sheriff, Mr. Pettibone here, can lay the perpetrators by the heels."

Mullins paused and looked around the room for effect. "What about this as a workable compromise? So long as the army demonstrates that they can, in fact, improve the protection of the public highways, we should have no objection to cooperation. Further, let a committee of responsible citizens be formed to whom reports can be made of suspicious actions. This committee can then pass judgment on the merits of each report before deciding whether to bring the information to the army's attention. This should satisfy Mr. Green's concern about harassment of private citizens, while at the same time filtering information so that the army's valuable time is not wasted in wild-goose chases.

"What do you say, Sheriff Pettibone? Is this a workable solution?"

Pettibone stood up next to Mullins, but given their difference in size, he appeared to be more dwarfed than ever when standing next to the storekeeper. He tugged on one end of his mustache reflectively and then commented, "It seems to me that that's a real workable answer, provided a' course that the right men be on that committee. What say you serve as the chairman, Mr. Mullins?"

Tom looked at his brother and raised his eyebrows as a low chorus of " 'At's right, Mullins'll keep 'em straight" and "Good idear" came from around the packed sanctuary.

Seeming flustered, Mullins clasped his hands in

front of him and bobbed his massive head up and down as his jowls quivered. "Why, I don't know what to say. I never considered . . . But if you think I should serve, why naturally . . ."

Matt Green, who was not altogether taken with Mullins, spoke up again. "I say put the parson on that committee. He's a man of sense, an' he don't talk so much!"

Parson Swift stood to acknowledge the nomination. "Thank you, Matt. I believe you all know that I can be trusted to keep your private thoughts private, but I do agree that something needs to be done to bring the murderers to justice."

"Who else?" someone said. "We need one more."

"Don't nobody suggest Matt!" another voice added.

Finally the parson spoke up again. "I'd like to recommend Jesse Dawson. He is a member of this community with a fine reputation. He has seen first hand the awful results of the crimes we're discussing, and he has a business relationship with the army which should make him acceptable to them. What do you say, Colonel?"

"A fine choice, Parson Swift, and a good solution all around. May I take it that the matter is settled then?"

There were nods of agreement mixed with some grunts of disapproval from around the room. Deputy Pettibone frowned, chagrined that no one had thought to recommend *him*. Noting his look, Mullins pointed out, "And naturally, Sheriff Pettibone's official capacity means that he will automatically be a part of the committee's discussions as we share information." Pettibone looked pleased.

The only other markedly unsatisfied individual was still sitting next to his brother as the men began to file out of the church. Tom leaned over and whispered to Jesse, "I can tell that this committee isn't your cup of tea. Why didn't you decline the *honor*?"

"I'm not sure I can explain why I let it stand. The parson's a good, level-headed man, but with Mullins being on the church board and all, I was thinking he might be able to throw his weight around." He grinned maliciously. "But maybe the parson and I can balance him some."

"You don't really think that committee will do any good, do you?"

"Maybe not, but the parson's right about one thing: I won't be forgetting the sight of that driver any time soon. Survived the wreck of the coach, and then stuck like a pig and left to bleed to death!"

———

Byrd motioned for Yancey to hurry. Yancey was far more adept and quiet at slipping through brush than Byrd and so had no difficulty keeping up. In fact, he reasoned, he could have followed Byrd from two hundred yards away.

The two were slipping up on the Dawson home in obedience to Mullins' instructions to kidnap Mont. Guidett agreed wholeheartedly with the plan since he saw it as a chance to recover what he believed was his rightful property.

Yancey had some misgivings. He expressed to Robert Mullins his doubts that any information Mont had would be valuable to them, and that kidnapping a child would arouse the countryside into a protracted search.

Mullins had snorted his derision. "For an orphan nigger boy? Nobody'll give him so much as a thought, much less try to search for him.

"And," the storekeeper went on, "if you do this correctly, everyone will believe the boy is a runaway and not kidnapped at all."

So Byrd and Yancey were now creeping down the Poso Creek draw, having left their horses about half a mile from the Dawson place. They had selected this night by watching for several evenings in a row from a hilltop overlooking the farm until what they were hoping for had occurred. Tom and Jesse Dawson had left together at the end of the workday to ride into Greenville, leaving Emily and the three boys home alone.

It was all well and good for Mullins to say that they could make it look as if Mont had run away, but if they were discovered, they wanted to avoid a gun battle or any possibility of pursuit.

The gathering gloom cast pools of shadows under the scrub oaks. Twice, coveys of quail flew out of the dust with a clatter of wings as they sought to escape the night prowlers by nesting in the tree branches. Overhead the bats darted in and out of the open spaces between the oaks.

At each disturbance, Byrd and Yancey stopped short and listened. No sound came from the direction of the farm except for the nicker of a horse accepting his supper.

Even Byrd began to walk more cautiously. He made an effort to avoid the piles of brittle buckeye leaves that the breeze had gathered into heaps.

They had circled behind the Dawson place so as to approach it from the uphill side. From the rising land to the west they could look down on the barn, which was completely dark, and on the house, where only a gleam of light was visible.

Byrd motioned for Yancey to squat down beside him as they prepared to observe for a while.

Almost immediately they were rewarded as they saw the door open and Mont walk out alone. He went across the dusty yard to the tack-room door of the barn and went in. A moment later, a light peeked through the cracks in the door to show that Mont had lit a lantern or a candle.

Byrd turned to Yancey and whispered, "Looks pretty easy, don't it? Yancey, you circle the long way around to the far side of the barn while I creep up on the corral-side closest to us." He added a few more instructions and then Yancey disappeared from view.

Byrd thought he saw movement behind the corral, but he wasn't sure. Minutes passed. Then he saw Yancey moving stealthily toward the far corner of the barn. "So far, so good," Byrd said under his breath.

The plan was simple. Yancey would approach the tack-room door and tap on it lightly as though he were Emily coming for a good-night word. As Mont opened the door, Byrd would grab him. Yancey was placed to block any bolt the boy might make away from Byrd's grasp. While Byrd held the child, Yancey would make a quick grab for Mont's meager possessions to complete the illusion that he had run off. Then they would ride back to the hideout.

Byrd began his stalk. First to the tree trunk nearest the corral, then to the corral's corner. From post to post he moved, a hulking shape of sinister intent.

At the corner of the barn he stopped. The next move was the most exposed since the front of the barn had no cover and was in full view of the house. Byrd noted with satisfaction that the barn door was ajar, giving him a halfway point to reach.

As he left his last concealment and made for the barn door, Byrd felt a rising excitement. It was all going so well. He'd have the boy *and* he'd show Mullins what he was capable of.

In the midst of his self-exaltation, he heard the front door of the house open. Someone was coming out. Instinctively his hand dropped to the butt of his gun, but he forced himself to jump into the crack of the barn opening and pull the door shut behind him.

He pressed himself into the shadows in the hinged corner of the crack and waited with bated breath.

It was Emily, and she was coming straight for the barn! Byrd examined her thoughtfully. As she reached the tack-room door and opened it, the light from within fell on her. Byrd could see her shape clearly. He liked what he saw.

Byrd licked his lips. *What a woman*, he thought. *Wouldn't I like—* His gaze lingered on her. *She's too good for the old clod-kicker she's married to; she'd prob'bly appreciate a real man like me.*

Byrd's lust began to overcome his caution. *Who's to know?* he thought. *Thar she is, not ten feet away.*

He had actually begun to move toward the door when he remembered Mullins' last command: "No one must know that anyone has the slightest interest in the child. If you cannot get away cleanly, wait for another occasion."

Byrd paused, his eyes narrowed, nearly deciding to disregard Mullins' orders. Then he heard Emily speaking.

"That's right, Mont. I've given the boys permission

to stay up until their father and uncle return. They'd like you to join them and play some checkers. Would you like to?"

"Oh, yessum, Miss Emily."

"Well, come on, then."

Byrd shrank back against the wall. *Blast it! We'll have to wait for another time,* he decided. *Then I'll grab the nigger, get that cussed Mullins off of my back, and have the woman, too.*

A moment more, and the door of the house opened and shut again as Emily and Mont went in.

Byrd whistled softly to Yancey and together they retraced their steps to where they had tied their horses.

When they reported their failed attempt to Mullins, he swore softly, but seemed relieved that there had been no disturbance. Byrd naturally didn't divulge any of his thoughts, but privately made his own plans for "another time."

CHAPTER 8

Tom and Jesse planned to look into Tommy Fitzgerald's tale of an old track around Shadow Ridge and the possibility of a cave there, but the farm delayed their exploration.

Mont worked eagerly alongside Nathan and Jed, helping with the haying and the digging of an additional root cellar to lay up potatoes, pumpkins and squash.

The boys were inseparable companions. They went exploring along the sandy banks of the level stretches of Poso Creek. Sent out to gather quail eggs and to search for late gooseberries, they would return just as often with a new variety of lizard or an unusually colorful feather.

Finally, the day came when Jesse and Tom felt free to go exploring. The boys asked to accompany them, but permission was denied.

"Boys, it's as rough a country as you'll ever see, even if it isn't haunted. Besides being steep and treacherous, it's a natural place for rattlesnakes and mountain lions." Jesse addressed himself firmly to his elder son. "Jed, I expect you to see that the littler ones don't act foolish or come to grief by being where they ought not be."

"Yes, Pa."

"Besides," added his uncle, who was tightening the

girth of his saddle as he spoke, "there probably isn't a grain of truth to the story anyway—more'n likely this will be a wasted trip."

"Boys, look after your ma while we're gone. Don't run off without fetching the water for the house and seeing that the woodbox is filled. We won't be gone over two days at most."

Tom went into his room in the barn and returned with his rifle. He thrust it into the leather scabbard hanging from his saddle, then went back for a powder flask and bedroll.

Jesse stepped away from his packed horse to where Emily stood in the doorway of their home.

"We'll be back soon, Emily. We'll just take a quick look around to see if what Tommy said was fact."

"I'll be praying for a safe and quick return for both of you," promised Emily, clasping Jesse's hands and looking up into his eyes.

"You aren't afraid, are you?" Jesse asked quietly.

"Not afraid exactly, no. It's more an uneasiness. If Byrd Guidett used a hidden trail like you think, then he murdered five people in cold blood."

"Emily, Tom and I aren't looking for a gun battle, and we'll go real watchful. I thought maybe you were believing the spook stories," he teased.

"Oh, hush and get on out of here! The sooner you two get this notion out of your systems, the sooner I get my new chicken coop built and the winter's wood split."

A quick embrace and a parting kiss, and Jesse swept into his saddle, even as Tom mounted Duncan.

"So long, Emily. See you, boys." With a last look and a wave they were gone, up the slope toward Shadow

Ridge, angling around its southeastern rim.

They rode easily at first, walking their horses up a hillside covered with scrub oak. Soon the gooseberry and manzanita patches grew larger and closer together.

Tom watched the ground for signs of a trail or even the marks that another rider had recently passed that way. He saw nothing to indicate the presence of anyone. The ground was thickly carpeted with decaying oak leaves, and he noted the clear impressions of deer tracks, and once where a bear had crushed the undergrowth.

Tom looked ahead to where his brother rode, and thought, not for the first time, what a fortunate man Jesse was. Tom admired him for what he had built, had carved out for himself. Emily had chosen well; Jesse was a fine provider and father for their family.

Only lately had Tom discovered in himself a desire to build. Always before his thoughts had run toward roving, seeing sights not seen before. Now he felt that the time had come to put down some roots.

Jesse turned in his saddle. "Don't you think we're wasting our time?"

Tom pulled his horse to a halt and pushed his hat back. "It sure appears so. Nobody's been on this stretch of hill in a hundred years, seems like."

Then squinting upward he added, "What do you say we split up and circle that granite face yonder? I'll try to work around the top and you push through that low spot."

"Even if we strike a path up there, that still won't explain how anyone could make their way down this slope without leaving so much as a trace. And to get down off this slope to the Poso Creek trail, they'd have to come through here someplace."

"You're probably right, Jesse, but since we're too late to head back tonight, let's camp up in the saddle anyhow and head back tomorrow."

Jesse examined the height of the sun above Shadow Ridge's rim and nodded his agreement. The two rode together for about a quarter of a mile; then Jesse turned his mount to pick his way down the slope, while Tom urged his horse up and around a sheer rock face.

Almost immediately, both men had trouble going forward. Jesse's travel was strewn with boulders—some big as wagon boxes—that had fallen from the granite wall. Bushy thickets had grown about the rock falls, causing him to backtrack often and look for a way around. Several times he found himself moving into what appeared to be an open space, only to find his line abruptly blocked and impenetrable.

Worse yet, the ground underfoot became treacherous, the soft earth giving place to shale rock, with only a thin layer of soil covering it. Jesse's mount began to pick its way along.

Jesse didn't urge it to any great speed, preferring to trust its sense of safe footing. This was a mountain-bred horse, no stranger to hillside trails. It had been called upon before to chase deer over rocky ledges and had gone down into and out of deep mountain canyons.

The horse plainly didn't like what it saw and felt on this stretch of Shadow Ridge. Gingerly stepping around a gooseberry patch that seemed to grow out of solid rock, the mount paused after each step to test its footing.

Meanwhile, Tom was having his own share of difficulty. On the first two places he approached, the upper

slope yielded dead ends against sheer granite outcroppings, and each time he had to turn farther back the way
they had come in order to proceed.

"At this rate I'll be home before we ever see the top
of this ridge," Tom addressed his horse. Duncan pricked
his ears to listen, then seemed almost to nod in agreement.

Rounding a house-sized boulder, Tom was surprised
to find a fairly open route up the face of the cliff.

Gaining the top of the granite escarpment in about
half an hour, he halted on top of a sheer drop to view the
countryside. Behind him the manzanita closed in, completely covering the saddle between the two nearest
peaks. It was apparent that no route over Shadow Ridge
could be found from this approach.

On three sides of him the land fell away, dropping
several hundred feet to the slope up which he and Jesse
had ridden, and then less sharply down to Poso Creek.

Tom could not see Jesse's ranch from this vantage
point, but he could identify the hill behind which it lay
and the bend of the Poso that contained Laver's crossing.

"Good lookout," he noted aloud, "or a place to signal
from."

Far below stretched chaparral and rockslides as far
as the eye could see. Tom mentally reviewed the possible
travel and concluded again that no trails were visible,
nor did any routes present themselves. Indeed, only one
rock-filled canyon cut through the mountainside, and it
provided no opportunity for travelers.

Tom observed that the canyon did intersect a bend
in the path of Poso Creek but at a point where the main
trail lay a few hundred yards away from the stream be-

hind a little oak-covered knoll.

"You know, Duncan, if a body could get down from here to that canyon's mouth, he'd cut off miles of trail and come out where he could choose his moment to set out on the road to Granite."

A further study of the canyon, however, indicated the impossibility of that thought since the gorge was both deep and narrow, except near its juncture with Poso.

"Now's when we could use Tommy's cave," Tom remarked. "Some way down past these slides and, say—"

Tom stood in his stirrups for a better view. A trick of light caused by the westering sun allowed something to appear to his eye that had not been there before. Right at the bottom of the gorge, only one bend of river from the Poso Creek intersection, was a large black shadow. A cave? A moment more and the hillside reverted to its previous appearance of gooseberry thickets and fallen buckeye branches.

Tom rubbed his eyes thoughtfully, but the shadow did not reappear, or rather, the lengthening shadows of the ridge swallowed up the canyon's mouth in gloom, eliminating the momentary contrast.

At that instant Tom heard a shot, followed by a shout. As if the mountain itself were falling, a roaring crash rose up, gaining momentum like peal after peal of thunder.

The horse snorted and pranced sideways as though suddenly fearful that the rock ledge underfoot would give way. Tom stepped from the saddle, shucking the rifle from its scabbard.

"Jesse! Jesse!" he called, even though he knew his voice would not carry over the echoing rumble that coursed down the mountainside and rebounded off the canyon walls.

Tom could see by a rising cloud of dust thrown up against the evening sky just where the rock slide had occurred. After two or three minutes that felt like hours to Tom, the crashing reverberations stilled, replaced by a soft sighing sound as if the mountain were settling itself. An occasional thumping crunch was heard as dislodged boulders bounded down the slope to find new resting places against the oaks far below. In another moment, all was silent.

"Jesse, Jesse, where are you?" Tom called again. But there was no answer, nor any further sound from that direction.

Catching up the reins, Tom jumped back into his saddle and began plunging down the slope he had lately ridden up. As though sensing his rider's urgency, Duncan plunged faster downward, leaping over boulders in his way and skidding across shale-covered slide rock.

When Tom regained the point at which he and Jesse had parted, he realized that picking his way around rocks and thickets would lengthen his travel, so he abandoned Duncan and followed Jesse's trail by foot.

Hurrying furiously, he scrambled over rockfalls in his path. A new rubble field lay at the bottom of the cliff, covering chaparral and manzanita thickets that had previously blocked forward progress at the cliff's base.

Rounding a corner of the granite outcropping, Tom tore through the thicket that remained, heedless of the barbed branches grabbing at his hands and arms, even piercing the leather chaps he wore.

Finally one more wrench free and Tom was in the

open. He stopped abruptly. There, at the cliff's base, lay his brother. Beside his outstretched hand lay his Colt revolver.

Tom rushed to his brother's side. Jesse was on his back, his face turned to the side. His clothes were not torn, not even disheveled. His hat was nowhere to be seen, but the hair across his forehead looked unmussed.

Tom knelt beside his brother. "Jesse, are you hurt?"

There was no reply, and as Tom gently turned his brother's face toward him, he saw the reason: the right side of Jesse's skull was crushed; he was dead.

Tom found Jesse's horse tangled in a thicket so that it could go neither forward nor back. From its location and that of Jesse's body, Tom surmised that the horse had bolted uphill, thus avoiding being buried by the slide, but unable to prevent the first falling rock from striking and killing Jesse.

———

The lengthening western shadows were countered from the east by a rising wind, but the sickly breeze did nothing to hold back the blackness.

Soon only the peaks of the Sierras held patches of sunlight on their heights. One by one even these tall candles were snuffed out.

Tom sat in the gathering gloom, cradling his brother's head in his lap. Tom's shoulders slumped and his neck bowed as if he were overcome with incredible weariness.

Twice he started up with a sensation of startled joy in the mistaken belief that his brother lived. Each time it was only a trick of his tear-blurred eyes that suggested movement—a ruse of the blood pounding in his ears that counterfeited breath.

A man cannot live long in the West without knowing death and its forms—sometimes peaceful, but more often sudden and frequently violent. Tom accepted the reality of his brother's death much the same way as the night fell—a few moments of lingering hope, and then black certainty.

He gave no thought to building a fire, having no energy to gather wood. He could hear the horses stamping nervously around, so he got up and unsaddled them, leaving them to graze. Then he returned to his lonely vigil.

The stars began to appear overhead, at first a handful, then hundreds, and later uncountable numbers as the Milky Way brightened into view. It was a moonless night, and the hazy starshine made all but the nearest bushes and rocks indistinguishable from the black hillside. Without the brightness of the moon, the stars appeared with more clarity and distinctness, distant as they were, than anything as near as the earth.

Tom's thoughts went back to his earliest memories of his brother. Mostly he and Jesse had fought. Jesse, the cautious, the thoughtful, the never-in-trouble one, and Tom, whom everyone thought first to blame when any mischief was discovered. And yet, there was always a deep-rooted affection between them, a sort of mutual admiration for the qualities the other possessed.

A night bird called from the brush, seemingly close by. The horses had settled down to cropping what dry grass they could find, and Tom knew that their natural caution on the steep slope would keep them from wandering far.

Tom was not by nature a fearful person, nor did the wild countryside at night hold any terror for him. Even the nearness of death made no impression of fear on him, and yet the night had an edge to it. An uneasiness penetrated his dulled senses as if part of his mind was keeping watch and sensing something amiss.

He tried to lay the blame for his jumpiness on his grief and his apprehension at the sorrow he would carry back down the mountain to Emily and the boys, but he was not entirely successful. His mind tried to reconstruct what had happened. He reviewed what he had seen of the rock face—the treacherous ground, the sudden crashing sound, the accidental discharge of Jesse's gun and his shout.

Something about the gunshot bothered Tom— something he couldn't quite put his finger on. Every time he tried to recapture the moment that perplexed him, his thoughts jumped to the tragic conclusion, and the ache he felt inside interfered with his reason.

He felt a rising anger, directed first at himself. Why were they up on this godforsaken mountain, anyway? There wasn't any trail and never had been. What was he trying to prove, and why, God, why had he dragged his brother along? Jesse, who lay dead on these stones, had never been adventurous, never courted danger. He should never have been overtaken by disaster. Why should he be dead while Tom still lived?

What would Emily do now? How could she raise the boys and keep the farm? The work was too much for one man, but they couldn't afford to pay a hired hand, so Jesse had sent for Tom.

What's more, Tom knew he couldn't stand to stay around. Emily would hate him, would hate the sight of him as a constant reminder that Tom had caused her loss. She and his nephews would sell the place and go to live with her family back in Missouri.

And Tom? He'd been wrong to think of settling down. He'd never be one to build anything or to own anything more valuable than his horse. He'd go back to drifting through the mining camps, or maybe he'd join one of the cattle ranches on the coast.

CHAPTER 9

It was altogether too fitting that the sky was a leaden gray with the first storm of the rainy season. The trees that stood guard over Oak Grove Cemetery still wore their leaves, but without sunlight to reflect from their surfaces, they appeared drab and subdued. Gray-ish-green moss hung in formless folds from their branches as if nature itself had put on a crepe of mourning.

The little group gathered around the mound of earth and the raw wound of a grave over which the pine coffin rested. The people in their black coats and black shawls stood silent and still, like an awkward group of statues.

All around were the graves of earlier settlers and their families. Some had reached this place of rest in ripe old age, and some in the bloom of youth. Their granite markers and lovingly tended plots mingled with rude patches of earth with dimly lettered wooden signs. These latter graves held mute testimony to strangers who had chanced to die or be killed in the hills; their epitaph was the sober phrase: "Known only to God."

Tom stood, hat in hand, beside Emily and opposite Parson Swift. The brothers braced their mother on either side, while Mont hung back. He felt grief, but was unsure how to express it, or even whether its expression would be welcome. Behind him stood a little knot of townspeople.

The parson reminded his listeners, "We have this treasure in earthen vessels, that . . . the power may be of God and not of us. We know," he said, "that if our earthly house were dissolved, we have . . . a house not made with hands, eternal in the heavens."

He went on to explain that because Jesse was a Christian, the parting that had taken place and the sorrow they felt, however strong and painful, was only temporary. He urged them to look around at the withered grass and remember that the same God who returned the green of spring each year would reunite them in new and glorious bodies that never felt pain or suffered death.

He prayed simply but with a firm voice for the Lord to help them through their grief, and asked that all present would be reminded of the fleeting nature of life and the need to "walk uprightly before their Maker."

When he concluded with a final "amen" and a chorus of murmured "amens" replied, Parson Swift moved around the grave to take both of Emily's hands in his. Looking at her with his kind blue eyes he said, "Emily, Jesse was a fine man. God has called him to some great purpose we don't see just yet, but I know your faith will bear you up—one day at a time." She nodded, unable to speak.

At a gesture from him, his wife came up from the group of mourners to take Emily's elbow and turn her from the casket toward those waiting to offer condolences.

Tom drew apart, standing alone now at the head of his brother's grave. A seething mass of emotions boiled inside him. Grief mingled with his sense of guilt was compounded by his swelling bitterness.

Parson Swift turned aside to speak with him, but before he opened his mouth, Tom burst out with, "Don't hand me any of your pious sayings, Parson! This needn't have happened. I don't care what you say about great purposes; Jesse's family needed him here!"

"Tom, don't you think God understands what you're feeling right now? Haven't we all felt at times like shaking our fist in God's face and demanding an explanation? But what other statement can He make than what He gave to Job, 'Where were you when I laid the foundations of the earth?' "

"That may be so, Parson, but if God caused this to happen, then I don't want any part of your God!"

"Tom, I won't pretend to have an answer that will satisfy you—but I know that God does, and I'll pray that He'll let you find it."

Among the group that gathered around Emily were many of the women of the community. Miss Peavy, the schoolmarm, expressed her sympathy, then drew Jed and Nathan to her and knelt to their height.

"Boys, you must be very strong and brave for your mother. Jed, you must be manly and look after your younger brother."

"And Mont, too?" added Nathan.

Miss Peavy looked perplexed for a moment, then turned to find a wide-eyed Mont James watching her fearfully.

"Well, I don't know. Now perhaps Mont will need to . . . Your mother may not be able to . . . what I mean is—"

"Noooo!" shouted Nathan. "Mont's *got* to stay with us, doesn't he, Ma?"

Emily looked around from where she was being embraced by Mary Davis, the livery stable owner's wife.

"Of course, Mont will stay on with us. Why should he leave now?"

"But, Emily, you'll have your hands full with your two boys and taking care of your place."

"Yes, and land sakes, Emily," added Victoria Burton, wife of the hotel's proprietor, "how will it look, you raising this black child as your own—I mean, well, he *is* black."

Emily looked confused. "But what difference can that make?"

"You're just not thinking clearly, Emily," said Mrs. Davis. "This child is part of that dreadful business about Byrd Guidett. Why, Jesse would be alive today if he hadn't gone off after that foolishness about Shadow Ridge."

"No, Ma, no!" insisted Jed and Nathan. "Mont didn't do anything wrong. Don't make him go away."

Tom could stand no more and burst into their discussion. Over his shoulder he called savagely to the parson, "Is this part of your fine God's plan too, blaming Jesse's death on this small boy?"

"No, it's certainly not," the parson said sternly. "Ladies, it is very unchristian and uncalled for at a time like this—"

"You have to talk like that, Reverend, but we all know what bad luck these niggers are. Just look at this war going on now! Why didn't we just leave them in their place?"

Tom was preparing for another outburst when a soft, oily sort of voice interrupted.

"I think that our emotions are all a little raw right

now, don't you, Parson?" Robert Mullins' carefully modulated tones dripped over his listeners. "I'm sure that Mrs. Davis is just expressing the frustration we all feel at the *eastern* war. Why, all of us have lost relatives in Mr. Lincoln's conflict, and this present tragic occurrence, accompanied by this Negro child, seems to bring us into that maelstrom somehow. Mrs. Davis certainly meant nothing personal. She was merely trying to suggest that the child's presence would be an unpleasant reminder. Perhaps it would be best if he stayed elsewhere for a time. With me perhaps. I could use some assistance around my store."

"Thank you, but no," replied Emily simply. "Mont will continue to stay with us for now. I'm sure he realizes that we don't hold him in any way responsible for what has happened."

She gathered up all three boys, and the group moved off toward the waiting buggies. She could not move quickly enough to escape the sound of the clods of earth falling on Jesse's coffin. Each man stepped up to the graveside to take a turn wielding one of the shovels. After a moment of silently turning the dirt, a nearby hand would reach out to take the shovel from its user before passing it on to another. As Mullins reached out to take the shovel from Tom's hand, the man murmured, "Terrible, terrible."

———

The service was over. The ladies of the church had prepared a meal for the family and friends to share back at the Dawson home. Each of the families represented separated at the gate of the cemetery to go to their respective homes, there to bundle up the savory meats and fragrant pies to offer as consolation to the bereaved.

Robert Mullins, the senior elder present, was in charge of locking the gate of the Oak Grove Cemetery. The last to leave, he paid his respects again to the family, shook hands all around with the other church members, and even had a moment's word with Pastor Swift about taking up a collection to provide a fine headstone for their recently departed brother, Jesse Dawson.

Nodding solemnly to each family as the buggies departed, Mullins looked the picture of respectability and Christian concern. He watched them disappear from sight around a curve of the road; then he raised his voice above its previous obsequious level and called, "All right, you two; you can come out now."

From behind a clump of brush on the knoll overlooking the burial ground stepped Byrd and Yancey. They walked down to meet Mullins where he stood beside the grave.

"Well, well. Once again a job half done. In case you didn't notice, there are *two* Dawson brothers, and one of them is still alive!"

As though he had been expecting this criticism, Byrd kept silent and let Yancey put forth their practiced defense.

"Now, boss, it's like this. When they split up on the hill up yonder, we know'd we could take one with the rockslide, see, and make it look an accident. As it is, ain't nobody thinks anything about ol' Shadow 'cept maybe it's haunted for true, and anyway it's powerful bad medicine. If we'd hauled off and shot that other one, somebody woulda gone to find 'em. Only then it weren't possible to make it be no accident—"

"You pitiful fools! Couldn't you have disposed of them in the tunnel where nobody would've been the wiser? Why should anyone have found the bodies at all?"

Byrd and Yancey looked guiltily at each other. Mullins had spotted the flaw in their excuse immediately.

Byrd figured that Yancey had not been as persuasive as he had indicated he could be, so Byrd himself decided to try.

"See, it was gettin' on to dark, and we wasn't gonna take no chance at lettin' Tom Dawson get away. But we figured it'd be worse to give away where we was for an uncertain finish than to send him down thinkin' it was an accident. We can finish with 'im later."

Mullins rubbed his face thoughtfully. "Why, Byrd, Yancey, you astonish me! I'd never have given you credit for coming to such careful restraint. This may work out for the best after all. There's clearly now no reason for anyone to explore Shadow Ridge any further."

Byrd looked pleased with himself. Completely ignoring the shake of Yancey's head, which was intended to mean *leave well enough alone,* he resumed explaining.

"Yes, sir, we know'd Tom Dawson would be comin' right wary, after that shot and all, and we—"

"What!" Mullins produced an almost piglike squeal. "What shot? I thought you said it entirely appeared to be an accident!"

"Now, jest calm yourself. The daid 'un only got off one round. We figger Tom'll put it down to a misfire when his brother's horse throw'd 'im. 'Course, it woulda been different if he'd nicked Yancey and we'd had trouble gettin' outta there our ownselves, but as it was—"

Mullins's voice and manner were icy. "You mean to say that Jesse Dawson saw you on the ledge about to push over the rocks and had time to get off a shot at you? You idiots! What if Tom figures out that it was no accidental discharge? What if the brother lived long enough to say something to him? You've already said it was near dark. How can you know for certain? Now we've got to eliminate Tom Dawson, and the sooner the better, before he has a chance to do any more thinking or to share his suspicions with anyone else."

"Cain't we jest dry-gulch 'im? Pettibone's no great shakes as a tracker. We could hole up on the ledge for a piece after."

"And have people start to question how it happens that two brothers both die so close together? We're trying to eliminate curiosity, not create more of it. Besides, have you forgotten about the black child? I can't afford to have you two in hiding for now—not after I've spent time leading Pettibone to think that the shooting of Colonel James was entirely self-defense."

Mullins paused, breathing heavily. "No, I've got a better idea. Let's go about this completely open. Everyone knows there's bad blood between you and Dawson over the nigger boy. What about if we set up another "self-defense" situation? Why, I'll bet I could even get awarded temporary legal custody of the child after such an unfortunate incident. Yes, broad daylight, that's the way of it." Mullins rubbed his hands together gleefully as though contemplating stacks of gold coins in his office safe.

Byrd's eyes narrowed and he ground out a question. "Ya want me to kill Dawson in front of witnesses and stand trial for it? You must be nuts. I ain't aimin' to get my neck stretched for nobody."

"There won't be a trial, you fool. Now listen; here's how we'll work it."

CHAPTER 10

The house was quiet now. *Too quiet*, Tom thought as he wiped his muddy boots and knocked timidly on the frame of the screen door. Behind him on the porch dry leaves scudded forlornly over the planks, then swirled away across the empty yard where only two weeks before, Jesse had wrestled playfully with the boys as Tom and Emily had howled with laughter. Tom stared hard at the place where they had tumbled down, and the memory almost made him smile again. But the vision was only a memory. The laughter and the moment would never come again, and that thought made Tom's smile die even as it reached his lips.

Mercifully, the boys had school to keep them occupied. Reading and writing, the mysterious world of ciphers, and childhood games could ease their pain a bit. But Tom and Emily had no such escape. The absence of the children only seemed to emphasize the terrible silence that had come to the ranch since the death of Jesse. That first dull ache of shock and disbelief was now honed into a sharp blade of grief that managed to pierce their hearts every time they turned around.

A thousand times a day Tom found a thought on his lips, but Jesse was not there to answer. Talk about the crops, the stock, the weather, and the war in the East was now suddenly frozen into a silent monologue. *What would Jesse think? What would Jesse do?* Those two questions had helped Tom reason his way through a maze of confused emotions over the last days. Jesse would want him to stay here as long as Emily needed help. He would expect Tom to see her and the boys safely back to Missouri.

Tom raised his fist and knocked again. He would tell Emily that. He would let her know he planned to do his duty by her and the children. For the sake of Jesse, he would see to it that they arrived in St. Louis safe and sound beneath her parents' roof. Emily's father was a wealthy man. He would see to it that his young, widowed daughter was well cared for. Emily was never meant to live a hard life in the West. She would fit in again easily with St. Louis society. Yes, he thought, she would fit. North and South, the country was filled with widows now as husbands clad in blue or gray shared common graves in places like Gettysburg. Wasn't that why Jesse had remained in the West long after the gold fields had begun to play out? Hadn't he remained here in California just so that he would not be forced to fight against friends and neighbors in this terrible war, so that Emily would never have to wear black or sleep alone in an empty bed, or call his name in the dark?

They had come west to escape the mindless destruction, and now, somehow, death had followed them even here. How pointless it all seemed! How unjust and harsh that the hand of God had swept across the face of the mountain, and—

The door opened. Emily's face was pale with grief but seemed to radiate an inner peace. "Why, Tom! What are you doing standing out here on the porch with your hat in your hand?" She smiled and held the door open for him.

He could not bring himself to look at her. Her black mourning dress had become the uniform that united the nation's women. It did not matter which cause their husbands, sons, or brothers had died for. Tom had never expected to see that uniform on Emily, however, nor could he have imagined that she would still be so beautiful even with the gingham and calico put away.

"I thought maybe we might need to talk a bit," he said haltingly.

"Yes. I was just going through—" Her eyes moved toward a neatly folded stack of Jesse's clothes on the dining-room table. "You and Jesse are . . . were . . . close to the same size, and I was wondering . . . Jesse would like you to . . ." She did not finish. Her voice trailed off as tears clouded her eyes.

Tom remained in the center of the room, toying nervously with his hat. He could not think of wearing his brother's clothes any more than of being able to fill his brother's boots. He cleared his throat. "No. No thank you, Emily. I . . . it might be hard for the boys to see me in their father's gear." He did not add that it would also be difficult for Emily. She seemed relieved by his reply.

"You're right. Silly of me. Then perhaps you could take them to Pastor Swift when you go to town? He'll see that they are put to good use."

Tom nodded in curt agreement, wondering how he could best broach the subject of selling the ranch and returning to the East. He glanced toward the desk where Jesse kept his journals and had spent hours long into the night deep in his accounts. "Jesse would want me to stay . . . I think . . . to help you." He cleared his throat again and scratched his head. "That is, if you would like me to, until—"

"Of course, Tom," she said softly, interrupting his words.

"We'll need to sell the place and then get you and the boys back home."

She drew in her breath sharply and glared at Tom as though he had slapped her across the face. "*Sell?* Back . . . you mean Missouri? Thomas Dawson! You can't mean that you think I would take my sons back to Missouri!"

Tom was instantly sorry that he had spoken. He had not meant to upset her, but he was in it up to his neck now. "Back . . . *home*, Emily. Your folks. Your family."

She raised her chin defiantly. "*This* is my home! This is where Jesse is buried, and one day I will be buried beside him!"

Tom ran his fingers through his hair. He should not have opened his mouth. He should have let her bring it up. She always was a strong-minded woman. "You can't stay here."

"You honestly believe that Jesse would want me to take our sons back to Missouri? Of all men, Thomas, I can't believe that you have forgotten that there is a war on! I have lost two cousins who fought for Georgia, and another who died fighting for Lincoln! Not only is the country divided, Tom, my own family is torn in two by this conflict. Missouri is a border state! Jesse had only just said to me how relieved he was that we are so far away from all that! How glad he was that the hand of God had brought us here to Shadow Ridge to raise our boys in safety and peace!"

Tears began to flow now as the words *safety* and

peace echoed hollowly in the empty house. She looked toward the pile of overalls and shirts sewn from flour sacks. Jesse had refused to exchange his mended denim for the uniform of a soldier. While others had turned in their plowshares for the weapons of destruction, Jesse had neither condemned nor joined them. When Tom had turned his back on the fighting and appeared at the ranch with tales of childhood friends firing from the opposite sides of a riverbank, Jesse had taken him in without a word of condemnation.

"When this war ends, Emily," he answered quietly, "I'll see to it you get back to St. Louis."

"Don't be such a fool, Thomas Dawson!" She whirled around to face him. "It doesn't matter who wins this war as far as you are concerned! If you go back to Missouri, you'll be hanged! And now you're telling me you're going back there!"

"Just to make sure . . ."

"To make sure there's still a price on your head? To make sure that both of the Dawson brothers die young?" Her fists were clenched as she hurled the absurdity of his thought back at him. "You don't have to go back to Missouri if you want to die young! Go back on that mountain! Back on that cursed mountain!" She began to sob now as she sank onto the settee. Blond hair fell in wisps around her face as she cried into her hands. "Do you really think this helps? Go away!" she cried. "Just get out, Tom. Let me be a while!"

Stricken, Tom stared at her in horror. What a fool he was! It was too soon to bring any of this up! Too soon! He backed toward the door. "I'm sorry, Emily," he said as he slipped out onto the porch.

The dry leaves swirled around his legs and followed

him back to his cot in the barn.

———————

Each member of the Dawson family chose a different way of dealing with grief. After Tom's unfortunate attempt to discuss relocating to Missouri, he took to finding reasons to go into town.

Jed alternately comforted and was comforted by his mother. He carried himself with a manly dignity and did his chores without being told. But when his mother brought him his father's pocket watch and said that it was right for him to have it now, he had to fight back tears and bite his lip. Emily found him later, sitting on the corral fence staring up at Shadow Ridge, the watch clutched in his fist.

Emily threw herself into housework. Given the excuse that many of their friends and neighbors would be dropping by to call, she found that the house could never be clean enough to suit her. She swept and scrubbed the wood-plank floors until they shone, and then was still able to locate imaginary crumbs to pick up. Alone at night in the empty bed, she couldn't sleep, so she took to rising at four o'clock in the morning, starting in again on chores that she had completed at midnight the night before.

Nathan, on the other hand, seemed to feel the weight of Jesse's absence the hardest—sobbing one minute, then becoming bitterly angry the next. Once when Tom returned from town, he happened to walk in and catch Nathan unawares. Nathan glanced up at his uncle, and the resemblance to his father was so great that the boy started up; then, realizing the deception, he ran crying from the room. Tom turned around and, without a word to anyone, rode back to town.

Nathan soon stopped playing with Mont. He did not intentionally ignore his friend, but he was unable to believe that his life would ever be the same again. With Jesse gone, there was no room for play.

So no one noticed how Mont was reacting to Jesse's death. He appeared at mealtimes, but they were such silent and unhappy affairs that he retreated immediately afterward to his quarters in the tack room.

———————

Daylight had begun to fade, and Emily was busying herself in the kitchen preparing a meal of cornbread and fried chicken. Tom had not yet returned from town, but supper was nearing completion, so Emily sent Jed out to the springhouse for a jug of buttermilk, and dispatched Nathan to fetch Mont.

"Mont. Hey, Mont! Ma says come to eat," called Nathan.

There was no reply.

"Mont, don'tcha hear me? It's time to eat." Nathan pushed open the tack-room door, a long creak of the hinges announcing his entrance. He expected to see Mont perched on the edge of his cot or seated in the middle of the floor repairing a piece of harness, but Mont was nowhere to be seen.

Maybe he's gone into the barn, Nathan thought, so he walked around the corner into the barn, calling for Mont all the while. A quick inspection of the stalls still gave no evidence of the black child's whereabouts.

Raising his voice to a shout, Nathan called out, "Mont James, come down from that hayloft! I don't want to play, and Ma's waitin' supper!" When there was no answer, he marched over to the ladder that led upward to the fragrant hay storage, the scene of many pleasant hours in happier days. Still no Mont.

Nathan was not worried, but he was perplexed and growing angry. It was not like Mont to be absent at meal-times. But then, Nathan couldn't remember having seen Mont at all since noon.

On the way back to the house, Nathan made a short loop past the corrals, the water pump, and the garden patch. No Mont.

"I'll bet he slipped around and went into the house when I was lookin' out here for him," reasoned Nathan.

"Ma," he called upon entering the house, "is Mont in here with you?"

Emily looked up from where she was filling a platter with pieces of chicken. "Why no, Nate," she replied. "Didn't you find him?"

"No, Ma, an' he's not in the barn, nor any place around."

"Perhaps he went with Jed down to the spring-house." No sooner were the words out of her mouth than Jed returned, carrying the jug of buttermilk, and without Mont.

"He wasn't with me," added Jed, having overheard their words. "And where's Uncle Tom?"

"Mercy me!" exclaimed Emily. "That must be the answer. He must have gone with Tom into town. They'll both be returning most any time now.

"You know, boys," she continued, "we must not forget about Mont no matter how bad we feel. We all have each other to lean on, but poor Mont has no family except us, and we must not shut him out.

"We all feel terrible just now," she went on, "and I

know that I haven't given you the attention I should have." She waved aside their protests. "But I looked around at the house tonight, and I think it's clean enough, don't you?" This brought small grins to the faces of the boys. "Let's make a pledge to start seeing, really seeing, each other again—and that includes Mont." She might have added *and your uncle*, but she didn't.

They were interrupted by the sound of Tom's horse outside but were so confident that Mont was with Tom that no one stepped out. A couple of moments elapsed while he unsaddled and turned Duncan into the corral. When he entered the house, he was alone.

"What's for sup—What are you all staring at? Is anything wrong?"

They all began to talk at once. "Isn't Mont with you?" "We can't find him." "Didn't he go with. . . ?"

When the din subsided, Tom looked to Emily for an explanation. "Tom, it seems that Mont is gone. I sent Nathan to bring him into supper, and he's nowhere around. The last time anyone saw him was at dinner today, and we thought perhaps he'd ridden over with you."

"Why no, Emily, I haven't seen him since this morning. You may remember, I left before noon. The last I saw of him, he was sittin' on his cot all by himself."

"Oh, Tom, that's just what the boys and I have been talking about! I'm afraid we've been neglecting each other—and Mont in particular. You don't suppose he's run away, do you?"

"Now, Emily, don't get all riled up. I'm sure he's around here someplace and hasn't come to any harm. The boys and I will go look for him right now. Okay, boys?"

The boys nodded vigorously, and soon all three had lit lanterns and gathered behind the house.

"Listen carefully Jed, Nathan. I want you two to go together. Head north to where Sandy Creek joins up with the Poso; and if you haven't found Mont by then, each of you get on either side of the creek and come down to Laver's Crossing. Don't get farther away than you can see each other's lanterns clearly. Don't go past the crossing; just turn and go back to the house. I'll meet you back there."

"Which way will you go, Uncle?" asked Jed.

"I'll head up Shadow Ridge way."

———————

Tom needn't have worried that the brothers would become widely separated. In fact, they traveled so closely together that one lantern would have been adequate.

The night was full of sounds—the familiar rustle of the long-tailed mice scurrying through the fallen leaves, the whisper-soft swoop of an owl's wings. Later on the mournful cries of the coyotes echoed from the summit of Carver Peak. The boys had no difficulty finding the juncture of the Sandy and Poso creeks, nor did they have any difficulty staying together. But they were not successful in finding Mont.

The lengthening search and the deepening night combined to stretch their imaginations. "Do ya s'pose he got snake bit?" wondered Nathan.

"Maybe," nodded Jed gravely, "or took off by Injuns more likely."

"Could be a mountain lion got 'im, or a great big ol' bear."

The same threat seemed to occur to them simultaneously. "You don't think . . . Byrd Guidett . . ."

———

Tom's search was all uphill. He moved in an arc, zigzagging back and forth across the slope and gaining a few yards of elevation with each swing. He tried not to think about his last trip down this hillside with the body of his brother, or how much he was coming to believe in the mountain's evil reputation. Of course, the more he tried to avoid these thoughts, the stronger they kept returning.

God, he thought, *aren't YOU supposed to be running things around here? First Jesse, and now this poor boy? Can't you make a better job of things than this? Here I am trying to get things settled at this ranch so I can take off and not be such a constant reminder to Emily of her sorrow, yet things seem to get more unsettled all the time!*

He was so lost in these thoughts that he almost missed exploring the little hollow formed by granite boulders and the fallen buckeye trunk.

Tom could never say later what it was that caught his eye. Surely no movement or flash of light—just the small dark clump that turned out to be Mont against the larger darkness. Tom jumped up on the buckeye log and raced into the rocky depression, calling out Mont's name. He began to fear the worst, saw himself carrying another corpse down to Emily—this time a slight little form. "God," he begged, "not again." And at that moment a very sleepy and bewildered Mont sat up and rubbed his eyes.

"Where is I? Mistuh Tom, is I gonna get beat?"

"Oh no, Mont. I'm so glad you're all right. You *are* all right, aren't you?"

"Yassuh, I'se fine."

"How come you're way up here on this mountain?"

"Well, suh, you and Miss Emily done been so kind to me an' all, an' now you is all so sad. Ain't no time to be alookin' after a no'count like me. Anyways, I heerd dem friends of Missy's say dat it weren't right for me to be livin' wid her no more, an' dat I'se de reason Mistuh Jesse got hisself killed. Anyways, I figgered she'd be better off if'n I went off . . . Maybe alookin' at me makes her sad mos' likely."

"Mont, nothing could be further from the truth. We all like having you around and don't want you ever to go away. Why, Nathan and Jed are out in the dark right now trying to find you."

"Is dat for true? Y'all wants me to stay?"

"I promise you, it's the truth. But say, weren't you awful scared up here by yourself tonight?"

"Oh naw, suh! I wasn't 'lone nohow."

"What do you mean, not alone?"

"You know, Mistuh Tom, Massa Jesus, He be right here beside me, so I'se got no cause to be scared."

There was a thoughtful pause; then Tom said slowly, "Mont, I want you to be my partner from now on. It seems that there are some things we can teach each other. For now, let's go home. We don't want to worry Miss Emily anymore, and I expect she's been keeping our supper warm for us."

CHAPTER 11

The Bella Union Hotel was not a fancy establishment, but neither was it a cheap saloon. A two-story affair that boasted decent food and clean beds for weary stagecoach travelers, it also attracted the business of some of the local families. Miners and cowboys, whose interests were more enticed by cheap liquor in less clean surroundings, would usually gather at the Diamondback or down at the Richbar.

So it was with some surprise that Scot McKenna noted the arrival of Byrd Guidett and Yancey into his place of business. They had been seen around town for the past few days and seemed to be minding their own business. An inquiry to Deputy Pettibone had brought the response that there was nothing Byrd could be charged with; if he caused no trouble, he was as free a citizen as the next man.

Byrd and Yancey went into the bar on the left side of the downstairs hallway, opposite the restaurant that opened on the right. McKenna watched from his place behind the counter, but made no move to interfere or question their presence. He produced whiskey and glasses without comment.

A moment later Tom Dawson walked into Bella Union, closely followed by Mont James. Tom and Mont had ridden over together to deliver Jesse's clothes to Parson Swift, and Tom intended to stop in for a drink before heading back. In deference to Emily's request, he sent Mont into the dining room for a lemonade rather than having the boy accompany him into the saloon.

Tom noted Byrd and Yancey seated at a table near the back of the bar, but he chose to ignore them. Instead, he stepped up and ordered his beer.

McKenna, like the name of his operation, was avowedly pro-Union. He and Tom fell to discussing the recent war news. Since the battle of Chickamauga, in which the casualties totaled almost forty thousand, the war had come to a virtual standstill. There had even been time to plan memorial services for those who had fought and died at Gettysburg. The dedication of the cemetery adjacent to the sleepy little Pennsylvania town was to have been scheduled for mid-October, but a conflict had arisen for the planned featured orator, Edward Everett, so the ceremony was postponed until November.

Neither man paid any attention when Yancey got up from the table and went out the back door.

A minute later Byrd rose to his feet and walked to the front window. "Hey, Dawson," he called, " 'pears to me yer horse is loose. Didn't anybody learn ya to tie a knot?"

Tom looked over. Sure enough, Duncan was trotting off down the street as if he had been shooed away from the rail. Tom knew the horse had been securely tied. Grimacing at McKenna, he went to retrieve Duncan, stopping by the dining room long enough to tell Mont to remain there till Tom returned. He figured that the horse would make his way down the street as far as the first livery stable, where he would stop in expectation of a handful of grain.

Byrd had remained at the window, and when he saw Tom going down the street to retrieve his horse, Byrd turned and entered the dining room.

"Hey, Nigger," he called to Mont, "come here a minute."

Mont looked scared, and said nothing.

"Are ya deef, Nigger? I said come here, an' this is a white man talkin'."

Mont still hadn't found his speech, but he could find his feet. He jumped up and ran for the back door of the Bella Union, then skidded to a stop as Yancey appeared in the doorway. Turning around, Mont tried to duck Byrd, who had followed close behind him. But Guidett grabbed the boy by the collar, picking him completely off the floor, then carried him into the saloon.

"Here, now," began McKenna, "what's this aboot? What'er ye aimin' to do with the boy?"

"Jest mind yer own business. This nigger was s'posed to belong to me, and I aim to get some work outta him.

"Here now, Nigger, suppose ya get on down there and shine my boots." With this he gave Mont a hard thrust to the floor. "What, no shine rag? I 'spect this'll do." He jerked Mont's shirt upward, ripping it apart and spattering the buttons, then threw the cloth at the boy.

"What? Nothin' to shine 'em with?"

Mont made as if to lick the cloth and apply it to Guidett's boot. Byrd kicked him in the stomach and chest, propelling him across the floor so fast he skidded into a brass spittoon, where he lay breathing in short, pained gasps. "How could ya even *think* such a thing, boy? Nigger spit on a white man's boot? You'd best think again, coon. Now, a white man's spit'd be proper for a white man's boots. Go on, reach on down in thar and get a big slug, then crawl over here and get to shinin'."

McKenna started to protest, but Byrd whirled around. "Jest keep yer mouth shut and yer hands on the bar. I'm collectin' on some winnin's, and I aim to get paid in full."

"Paid in full sounds like a lot to expect from a small boy, Byrd Guidett. Perhaps your account would get settled more to your satisfaction with me." Tom Dawson had returned and stood in the door of the saloon. He had taken in the scene at a glance, and his hand hovered near the Colt that hung at his side.

"Are ya fixin' to draw against me, Tom Dawson? Takin' the part of a nigger against a white man—why, some folks'd be callin' you a nigger lover."

"Call me anything you like, Guidett, but touch that boy one more time and they'll be calling you dead."

Yancey moved crablike around the side wall till he was even with Byrd on the other side of the room and also facing Tom.

Byrd made as if to step forward and kick Mont again. His expectation was that this would goad Tom into drawing, and Byrd believed himself to be the better gunman. He also knew that McKenna could truthfully report Tom's threat; and in this community of largely pro-Southern sentiment, a verdict of self-defense would easily be obtained.

What he did not expect was that a very determined small black boy would see the kick coming. Grabbing the spittoon, Mont hurled it and the contents into Byrd's face.

"What the—?" Byrd clawed at the slimy goo that clung to his face and beard. He dared not lash out now, or attempt to draw, for he could only dimly see through the tobacco juice that burned his eyes.

Tom had indeed drawn his gun, but he swung it to cover Yancey, who put both his hands up slowly and backed against the wall.

"Mr. McKenna, will you be so kind as to remove Mr. Guidett's weapon? Thank you. Now, if you'll please hold it on his friend over there. I wouldn't want anything to interfere with Mr. Guidett's receiving a full accounting of what he is owed."

So saying, he released the hammer of his own gun and, calling Mont to him, gave it to the boy to hold.

A wild look of delight spread over Byrd's face as he guessed Tom's intention. "I'll break you in two!" he screamed and lunged at Tom.

Tom sidestepped the jump easily, and Byrd plowed past him like a runaway locomotive, crashing into a table. Whirling around, Byrd made as if to jump at Tom again; but this time as Tom moved to one side, Byrd also pivoted and grabbed Tom's arm.

Pinning Tom's arms to his sides, Guidett lifted his adversary off the floor bodily in a massive bear hug. This was Byrd's favorite move. With it he had crushed men's ribs and made them cry for mercy before he allowed them to crumple to the floor. But he had not reckoned with the wiry strength of Tom's arms and shoulders as he flexed his muscles and pushed Byrd's embrace away.

In the slack thus obtained, Tom leaned his body backward in Byrd's grasp, and then bent it forward suddenly, ducking his head. He drove the top of his forehead directly into Guidett's nose. With a scream of infuriated pain, Byrd dropped his hold and grabbed his face with his hands. His nose was gushing blood.

Tom followed up his advantage by driving his right fist into Byrd's midsection. This blow made Byrd back up a step, but as Tom closed in, Byrd raised his two clasped hands over his head and brought them down with a hard thrust, striking Tom over the left ear so hard he staggered back.

Byrd gave a wild cry, his face a fearful mask of gore and tobacco juice, and brought both his fists together on either side of Tom's head. Tom stumbled, his head spinning. Seeing his advantage, Byrd closed in, intending to apply his crushing hug again.

Tom knew he couldn't escape that clutch as easily this time, so he moved to step in toward Byrd at the moment when the cutthroat's arms were outstretched to encircle. Not expecting anyone to deliberately come within his reach, Byrd was unprepared to ward off the blow from Tom's left. It worked even better than Tom anticipated, for as Byrd raised his head to apply his press, Tom's fist caught him in the throat.

Byrd backed up, gasping. He couldn't breathe through his nose, and now his throat felt paralyzed and his eyes were swelling shut. He had to work fast. Again he threw himself at Tom, and this time Tom was unable to avoid the rush. Byrd's force hurled him back savagely against the counter of the bar, making him cry out at the stabbing pain from a breaking rib.

He tried to slip under Byrd's grasp, but Guidett followed him down to the floor, then jumped up for a leap that would land both his knees and all his weight on Tom's chest.

In that split second, sensing Byrd's gathering force

preparing to spring, Tom reached out wildly with his arms and encountered the spittoon lying where it had rolled after being thrown by Mont. Tom's fingers closed over the rim, and in the next instant he drove it with all his remaining strength against the side of Byrd's head. The impact snapped Byrd's head against the bar, sending a shower of blood through the air.

The force of this strike was not great, but it was enough. Guidett had had difficulty breathing since the blow to his throat, and now he collapsed on top of Tom.

For a moment, neither moved. Mont was crouched on the floor, biting his lip to keep from whimpering. Yancey slouched against the far wall, casting wishful glances toward the exit—a thought which McKenna discouraged with a negligent wave of the gun. Finally, Byrd Guidett stirred, and a muffled voice underneath croaked, "Get this stinking mess off me—I'm about to be crushed!"

"Remove Guidett," directed McKenna to Yancey, "and mind that ye drag him face up, so ye get no more blood on me floor!" Yancey instantly obeyed, pulling the ugly heap away. By the time he had dragged Byrd to the front porch, he began to revive. Yancey helped the man to his feet and two staggered outside, where he doused Byrd's swollen face in the nearest horse trough.

McKenna insisted on helping Tom personally. He made him sit in a chair while the barman rubbed a towel soaked in whiskey over cuts on Tom's ears, forehead and knuckles, while muttering to himself, "This is better than that nasty carbolic, and smells nicer, too."

Tom tried to rise, but a stabbing pain in his back made him gasp and sit back down. McKenna helped Tom remove his shirt, then bent him forward gently. "Ay, he's broke one o' yer short ribs, lad. 'Tis a good thing ye're as strong as an ox, or he would have crushed yer whole ribcage like an eggshell. As it is, ye'll be mighty tender for a spell, but ye'll soon be right as rain. Here, boy"—this was addressed to Mont—"run upstairs to me room, 'tis the one jist at the top, and bring a sheet off me bed."

Mont looked first to Tom for permission, and at his nod, ran upstairs. He wasn't sure what drew him to the window, but stepping past McKenna's rumpled bed, Mont looked down into the street. What he saw there puzzled him, for he noticed a most unlikely conference. Mont saw Byrd get up from the horse trough and shake his head like a dog shakes water from its body. Then he turned as if to reenter the Bella Union, violently throwing off Yancey's restraining hand. Next Mont saw the two seemingly being addressed by someone on the boardwalk in front of the hotel. It looked as if Byrd started to argue, placed a boot up on the step, then stopped. A moment later, Byrd and Yancey turned to walk down the dusty street leading out of town, with Byrd turning back twice and Yancey urging him along. But the one who had apparently ordered them out of town stayed out of Mont's view.

Mont returned with the sheet. McKenna tore a strip from it and, directing Tom to hold it under his arm, proceeded to wrap him around and around until, in Tom's words, he was "trussed up like a turkey."

"Do you have to make this so tight?" Tom complained. "I was having enough trouble breathing as it was."

"Ay, lad, 'tis for yer own good. We can't have that bone wanderin' around in ye. Give this but a week or so to knit, and ye can unwind it. Then ye'll be ready to fight again . . . And what a fight it was! I know of no man who's stood up to Byrd Guidett and lived." He picked up the spittoon, now completely concave where it had connected with Byrd's skull, and shook his head ruefully. "A perfectly good spittoon ruined, and him still alive after, more's the pity."

"Yes, well, I only wanted him to leave Mont alone. I'm glad I didn't have to kill him to teach him that."

"Ye may regret it later. Byrd's head is hard in more ways than one, and he'll not like bein' bested in a fight. Ye'd best watch yer back trail, and keep yer wits aboot ye."

CHAPTER 12

Byrd waited until he judged that the last of the late arrivals had come. The hillside from which he watched not only overlooked the church but also gave him a view in both directions through town.

It was a frosty morning; his breath, as well as that of the bay horse on which he sat, was visible in ragged, steamy puffs. A fitful, lusterless sun was trying unsuccessfully to break through the overcast. It contributed no warmth to the day, only the promise that it would stay just above freezing.

The horses in the churchyard stood huddled together in little clumps for warmth, even normally fractious ones subdued in spirit. A row of horses still hitched to buggies and wagons stood in a row, tethered to a cable string between two iron bolts in adjacent oaks.

I'll show those crackers how it is, Byrd thought, feeling his battered nose.

Occasionally he could hear the pump organ straining to produce a hymn, but with the doors and windows tightly shut against the cold, the sound was muffled. Byrd could not be sure that all the occupants of the church building were unarmed, bundled up as they were in heavy coats, but he considered it unlikely that any carried firearms.

"Too bad for them if'n they do," he muttered sarcastically.

He couldn't see Yancey from where he waited, but he knew Yancey was watching him. "I'm blasted if'n I'm gonna freeze my tail out here any longer," he mumbled to his horse. "Let's get this show on the road." He stood in his stirrups and waved his arm three times over his head.

Yancey broke from the cover of the creek bed next to the church property, and covered the small slope to the building in a stiff lope. Both men knew that Yancey's approach could not be seen from any of the church windows. Yancey waited to the side of the church's front doors and at the bottom of the steps, where he could duck around the corner and out of sight if anyone unexpectedly appeared.

Now! Byrd thought, adjusting his mask and drawing his Colt. He urged the horse down the hillside until at the bottom it was in direct line with the church door. "Eyowhh!" he yelled, and drove his spurs into the bay's sides. The startled horse leaped forward, bolting across the road, while Byrd fired three shots. His first went into the air, but his second and third bullets went through the upper panes of two of the tall church windows.

He was at the steps, where Yancey had already flung open the doors and ducked back to the side. Byrd's excited horse never even hesitated but jumped up to the entrance in one bound, then past the doors and into the building itself. Byrd had to duck to keep from getting knocked off by the doorframe, but he came up shooting; everyone else in the building ducked, too, crying with fear as they dived for cover.

His next shot took out another window; then in a

flash of devilish inspiration, he took deliberate aim at the smokestack of the potbelly stove standing in the center of the twenty-by-thirty room. With a crash and a clang, the pipe parted at the joint nearest the ceiling, showering soot on everything. The pipe folded up on itself as if exhausted from having stood so long, then collapsed into the center aisle. Grayish-brown smoke poured from the stove into the little room, only the high ceiling prevented the scene from being instantly obscured.

Byrd next turned his attention toward the pump organ at the left front of the room where a slight gray-haired lady had been playing. He shot the last bullet in the revolver directly through the side of the instrument, which erupted in a clatter of keys and stops, then gave the groan of a dying cow. The organist leaped backwards off the organ bench. There she cowered—a rumpled heap of skirts and wounded dignity.

Byrd transferred the empty weapon to his holster and drew another from his belt. Circling the prancing horse in the space between the door and the ruined stovepipe, he noted with satisfaction that all the women were huddled down between the pews, covering the heads of small children, and that not a few of the men had ducked under cover as well.

In this first moment of shocked silence, Parson Swift, who had been seated on the small platform behind the pulpit, rose to his feet. "What's the meaning of this outrage?" he demanded.

"Shut up and sit down, you old Bible-thumper! I'm here to deliver a message, an' it won't hurt my feelin's none to shoot you first!" So saying, he cocked the pistol and deliberately leveled it at the preacher's chest. "An' that goes for any of the rest of you what feels like inter-ruptin' me!" His voice croaked awkwardly.

"This here message is to any folk what feels like lickin' them Yankee soldier boys' boots. Don't do it! They may think they got a lock on this state, but they got another think comin'! We aim to make them Yankees think that their hides'd be a whole lot safer outta these hills for good, an' that goes for any other nigger lovers in these here parts! An' don't count on no blue-bellies to protect ya; they cain't even protect their ownselves!"

Looking right into the muzzle of the gun, the parson said calmly, "Are you quite through?"

Byrd's pistol remained pointed at the parson for an instant longer; then whirling his horse around, he gal-loped out the door and down the steps, firing three more times as he did so.

———

The waters of the little cove were so deep that the dark blue color of the Pacific Ocean did not lighten at all as it swept up against the rocky headland. The small peninsula was covered with cypress trees, which further sheltered the south-facing bay from storms.

On shore a smoky fire was burning, producing a thick, greasy plume that reached up into the afternoon sky. Beached in the cove was half a carcass of a gray whale, the other half having already been drawn up the short slope to the try pots. The teams of mules that pulled the fifty-foot-long strips of blubber balked when first introduced to the smells and sights of the whaling station; but they soon discovered that the footing was more sure and the loads easier to move than the cinnabar ore they had lately been hauling on steep mountain paths.

Robert Mullins didn't believe he could ever get used to the sights and smells. The oily film that covered everything in the area disgusted him, and the view of the partially stripped whale with its ribs exposed and its blood coagulating in little pools on the shore was obscene.

And this rube of a captain is not cooperating, either, thought Mullins.

"Captain Alexander," Mullins tried again, "I really need your assistance. You have been recommended to me as a trustworthy individual whose sympathies are all correct. Surely you can see that the transportation of arms from San Francisco could be accomplished much more easily and safely from this point on the coast to the central mountains than overland past the many forts of the valley."

"I'm certain that what you say is correct, Mr. Miller," replied the captain, unaware of Mullins' real name. "But why come to me at all? I merely operate this whaling station for Mr. George Hearst, who owns this ranch. I'm not an arms merchant nor a shipper of arms. I came to this coast to get away from the cussed war and ply my trade in peace. As you can see," he said with a sweep of his hand, "I only make war on whales."

Mullins replied calmly enough, although inside he fumed like the try pots, "I've shown you the cuff links and explained how I came to have both of them. I've also shown you that I can pay. What more do you need?"

Alexander pulled his hat down over his forehead until its brim almost touched his hawklike nose, and he gazed sternly down at Mullins. "I've heard your story, all right, and I concede that your tale about one of your hirelings having mistakenly killed Mr. James in a drunken brawl is too wild for any pea-brained Yankee to have concocted.

"Nevertheless," he continued, "Mr. James should have had in his possession certain information that would confirm your status and sustain your worthiness to be privy to the name of my associate in San Francisco."

"I've already explained that we know how to locate the papers. It's merely a matter of doing so in a way that will avoid unnecessary interest on the part of federal agents."

"I applaud your caution, Mr. Miller, but its very fact should help you to understand my position. You say that you want to arm some miners who will seize the gold production for the Confederacy and then throw the Unionists out of the valley. Even if such a program were of interest to me, you must understand that there are larger wheels turning in the world than your little machinery. Plans are at work to deny the northern oppressors the use of any ports on the Pacific coast. Do you catch my drift?"

"Indeed I do, Captain, indeed. But can we not begin now to work toward that glorious day, and the inclusion of California in its rightful place under the Stars and Bars?"

"Not without your papers, Mr. Miller. You must have those papers!"

———————

The two boys darted eagerly from tree to tree in their play, swooping and turning like a pair of swallows in flight. The morning was perfect for play; clear and crisp after the first snow of the year had left only an inch or two of pure white powder on the ground. The snow would not remain past noon; indeed, it had already slipped from the tree branches, but right now was a perfect time to practice tracking skills, mingled with a rousing game of hide-and-seek.

Nathan and Mont might have missed having Jed around if they'd stopped to think about it. But for the time being they were having too much fun to regret that the older boy, who was usually their leader, was home with the measles.

"He must rest quietly, boys, and he can't do that with you whooping around the place, so off you go. Besides, if you catch the measles, you'll have to be quiet soon enough yourselves, so get out and get to playing," Emily instructed.

They hadn't needed much urging.

"Look here, Mont, this is a rabbit's track. An' over here, slippin' up alongside Mr. Rabbit, is an ol' fox."

"I hope's Mr. Rabbit done made it home safe," commented Mont.

"Me too. An' lookit, see where this deer went by. Lessee, he stood right here nibblin' on this bush. Then somethin' musta spooked him; look at the jump he made. Clean over here, and then off he run!"

They moved from discovery to discovery throughout the morning as if the world were newly created for their enjoyment. At the juncture of Sandy Creek, they turned to follow its course mountainward into newer and less familiar territory. Presently they came to a gooseberry thicket, where a few little runways already imprinted in the snow gave evidence of the passage of a flock of quail.

From the center of the thicket a soft clucking, churring sound could be heard.

"My pa always says, said, he . . ." choked Nathan, and his voice trailed off.

"Go on," urged his friend gently. "What he done said?"

Nathan drew himself up proudly. "My pa said that on cold mornin's or right after a snow, the quail family always stays close to home. See, they get right in the middle of their patch of berry thorns; they keep each other warm, and they stay good and safe that way."

"Your pa was sure enough a smart man, an' a kind one," observed Mont, "an' he made me feel right ta home wid you'uns. Jes' like the li'l quail mus' feel in de middle of his fambly."

Nathan nodded sadly. "I miss him somethin' fierce, Mont. Sometimes I forget that he's gone, and I think of somethin' I want to run and show him, and then I remember and. . . . Anyways, I like rememberin' things he taught me. When I tell 'em to you, it makes me feel better somehow, almost like he was here himself.

"Say," Nathan brightened, "I'm gettin' hungry. How 'bout you? Ma packed us some lunch, but I reckon that we could have part of it now and save the rest for later."

"Sounds mighty fine to me. What we got?"

Nathan rummaged through the burlap potato sack he had been carrying slung over his shoulder. "Let's see, here's some cold chicken and a piece of cheese each and an' some crackers. An' here"—he paused for effect—"here's provisions for us mighty trackers. Brown sugar and butter sandwiches!"

The two boys sat back-to-back on a boulder at the head of the gooseberry patch, where they could see part way down the valley that was their home. The fresh-baked bread was thickly sliced and spread with home-churned butter. The brown sugar filling made a crunching sound in the still morning air, and the delicious sweet taste complemented their camaraderie.

When they finished eating, Nathan suggested they get their game of hide-and-seek underway. "Now, we need some boundaries."

"What's a boun'dree?" inquired Mont.

"You know, markers to show how far you can go to hide so's the game is fair. Like, let's make this rock the farthest up this hill you can go, and the creek down yonder is the bottom. On the east side we'll say"—he paused to study the terrain with a judicious eye—"that there big cedar tree, and on the west that pile of rocks yonder."

"Whar's safe?"

Nathan carefully inspected again. "It needs to be somewhere's right in the middle. I know. You see that bunch of ol' buckeye trees all twisted around together? Right in the middle of that."

"Who's gonna be 'it' first?" asked Mont as they walked down the hill toward the clump of buckeyes.

"Let's peg for it. First one as can stick this Barlow knife in that buckeye trunk gets to choose."

Nathan produced his pocketknife, and the two took turns trying to make it stick in the twisted wood. On his third try, Nathan succeeded. "All right, you hide first an' I'll seek. We'll leave that knife there to mark home. I'll count to fifty, an' then I'll come lookin' for you."

"Make it a hunnert," begged Mont. "I wants to hide real good!"

"All right, a hundred it is," replied Nathan. So saying, he turned his face to the tree trunk and began counting loudly: "ONE, TWO, THREE . . ."

"Count slower!" Mont yelled back over his shoulder as he circled once around the clearing, hoping to confuse his pursuer before striking out to the west as quietly as the scrunching snow permitted. Once he stopped to throw a rock back into the middle of a brush pile; then he turned to run on, chuckling quietly to himself at the trick he was playing on his friend.

Mont knew exactly where he was headed, for the westernmost "boundary" of rocks had attracted his attention while they were eating. Directly in front of the heap of boulders an oak tree had fallen across a buckeye, and the two trees had crashed to the ground together. The gnarled buckeye, being all twists and turns, would not lie flat, but made a little archway over which the branches of the oak spread a partial cover.

As he approached his chosen hiding place, he slowed, even though behind him he heard "eighty-five, eighty-six . . ."

Mont selected his path carefully now, leaping from a rock to a pile of brush and from the brush to a clump of gooseberries and from there to the oak's trunk, and then down behind it into the space left vacant by the buckeye's fall.

Mont stood for a moment, noting with satisfaction that he could see no footprint nor any other sign of his passing in the last hundred or so feet of his path. *'Spec that'll pause 'im some*, he thought, as he settled down to wait.

Nathan was just finishing his count. "Ninety-nine, one hundred! Ready or not, here I come!" So saying, he took off directly east, toward the sound made when Mont had thrown the rock. Since Mont had circled around that way before taking off west, Nathan was supported in his choice by the sight of Mont's footprints in the snow.

I'm hot on his trail already, thought Nathan. He jumped up on a chunk of granite to survey the scene for possible hiding places. South and east he noticed a clump of brush that looked promising, and set off in that direction. He remembered to watch over his shoulder in case he was wrong and Mont broke from cover to run for "home."

Nathan skidded to a stop in front of the brush pile. Carefully he circled it, looking for Mont's tracks before his own had obscured the trail. All around the suspected hiding place the ground was clear and covered with a blanket of unmarked snow. Nathan stopped to scratch his head in thought. *He can't have come this way unless he flew.* He spotted a nearby scrubby oak with a fork about eight feet off the ground, and decided to try it as a new observation post.

Mont poked his head ever so carefully up from behind the buckeye and heard Nathan moving off to the east. He had just about decided to risk a dash toward the embedded knife when he saw Nathan climb up the oak, and from his perch in the cleft of the tree, begin a slow scan of the countryside. Quickly, Mont ducked back down.

Nathan had noticed the jumble of buckeye and oak, but from his angle, there didn't appear to be any space that offered a hiding place. Instead, he decided that a growth of manzanita over near the cedar that marked the eastern edge of their game looked promising. He jumped clear of the tree into a little pile of snow at its base and ran off to investigate the new possibility.

Mont remained hidden. He couldn't tell if Nathan

had left his lookout or not, but he didn't want to offer any movement as a target. He amused himself by making a little pile of stones behind the log, all the while listening carefully for the sounds that would indicate his friend was approaching. Presently, he heard them. There was the sound of boots crunching on snow and a sharp crack of a branch breaking underfoot. Mont huddled down into the hillside, trying to breathe even quieter and willing his pursuer to go away. Mont strained his ears, but no longer could hear Nathan's footsteps. Had he succeeded in fooling his friend?

Mont eased his cramped legs just a little and thought about raising up once more to survey the hill. At that moment, a sound from behind him made him freeze. Then right over his head a booming voice exclaimed, "Wal', what's this here? If it ain't a runaway nigger, catched at last!" A brawny hand grasped Mont's coat collar and lifted him bodily out of concealment, then turned him around in midair, bringing him face-to-face with the sneering face of Byrd Guidett!

Mont kicked and struggled and tried to scream, but a huge hand clamped over his mouth, and all his efforts only got him a clout over the ear with another heavy fist.

Nathan had explored all the area around the eastern boundary. He thought about climbing another tree, but none close by had branches near enough to the ground for this to be done easily. Remembering what he had seen of the fallen trees, he put his hands together in a quick gesture of anticipation. "Sure enough, he's fooled me! Why I bet he's fixin' to make a dash for home right now."

With this thought, Nathan began running as fast as he could back across the area of their play. When he reached the tree with his pocketknife stuck in it, he was pleased that Mont hadn't gotten there ahead of him, so he continued on toward the west.

Nathan rounded the end of the oak's stump at full speed and almost collided with Byrd, who was threatening Mont with another blow if he didn't stay still. Seeing Nathan he exclaimed, "What's this? Another one?"

"Let him go!" Nathan shouted at Byrd. "You let my friend go!"

"You jest come on over here to me, boy. I'm jest havin' a little talk with this nig . . . I mean, yer friend here. Whyn't ya join us?"

Mont twisted free for an instant and called out, "Run, Nathan, run!"

Nathan took one more look and decided that getting away to get help was the best he could do. He turned to make a run for his house, but hadn't gone more than three steps when Yancey stepped out in his path with his boot knife in his hand. "You'd best do as the man says, and walk on over thar nice and easy like. It ain't real comfortable tryin' to run with this here knife astickin' betwixt yer shoulders, so ya'd best walk nice and slow."

"My uncle is coming to get us. He should be here any time now. You'd better let us go right now."

Nathan's attempted bluff was good, but it had the wrong effect. Yancey looked at Byrd and raised his eyebrows. "Could be the boy's tellin' the truth. Stead of tyin' him up, what say I jest cut his throat and be done with it?"

Mont stiffened in horror in Byrd's grasp, and Nathan stood rooted to the spot, too frightened to run, when Byrd replied, "Naw. That'd raise the whole countryside after us. If we ain't got time to tie 'im to a tree, we'll jest have to take 'im along. There ain't nothin' here to show they was around anyways, so no one will know what's happened to 'em nohow."

Yancey's lips parted in a sinister grin. "We got 'em, Byrd. We finally got 'em."

CHAPTER 13

Like a deer carcass across the saddle bow, Nathan hung head downward over the horse's withers. They were moving at a fast trot—deliberately, not in headlong flight. The bouncing motion with the saddle horn in his stomach made it hard for Nathan to breathe. Even if he hadn't been scared to death of Yancey's knife, he wouldn't have been able to yell for help. Nathan tried to concentrate on getting air into his tortured lungs and after that to pay attention to the direction of their travel. He could tell that they were skirting the edge of Carver peak and moving along parallel to, but some distance from, the side of the trail that led to the mining town of Tailholt.

Nathan tried to think what would happen to them. He believed that his uncle would come in search of them if they weren't home by nightfall. But they hadn't left any word about which direction their play would take them. Nor had they been able to leave any sign showing where they had been. Even if Tom located the trail of the two horses, how was he to know that it had anything to do with the disappearance of the two boys? Nathan began to pray silently, *Dear God, help us!*

Mont, meanwhile, was unconscious. He had attempted to struggle in Byrd's grasp, then tried to persuade the outlaws to release Nathan. But all he got for his efforts was a gruff "shut up!" from Byrd and a clout alongside his ear that had knocked him senseless. Byrd's grip kept the boy from falling headfirst to the ground.

The two outlaws drew up at the head of the canyon that sloped down around the northern flank of Shadow Ridge toward Tailholt. "Shall I kill 'em and dump 'em here?" asked Yancey, indicating the trembling Nathan.

"Naw, this is too close to our real track, an' anyways, Mullins may know of some use for the brat. Jest you be sure of this—" Byrd addressed Nathan by sidling his horse up close and yanking Nathan's head up by the hair. "If'n ya cause us any mite of trouble, ye're nothin' but crowbait. Is that right clear to ya, boy?" Nathan gave the tiniest of nods at Byrd's scowling face, and then his head was flung back down to bounce off the horse's shoulder.

Yancey motioned to the trail. "What say we split up here, jest in case Dawson do get after us?"

Byrd felt his nose and head for a moment, then re-marked, "Maybe I been lookin' at this thing all wrong. I got a real hankerin' to meet up with Tom Dawson again. Maybe I oughta go on back an' make it easy for him to find me!"

For a moment Yancey looked genuinely worried that Byrd's temper and his desire for revenge would result in their getting caught. He thought for an instant, then re-marked carefully, "You could sure 'nuff do that, Byrd, but we better not wait on gettin' that darkie to tell us where them papers is hid. You already know what an uproar Mullins is in. Jest hold on for a bit. You'll get yer chance soon."

Guidett looked as if he wanted to argue, but apparently saw the wisdom of Yancey's advice. He indicated with a jerk of his head that Yancey should take the right side of the canyon, while he and the still unconscious Mont rode down the left.

Now Nathan was more confused than ever. *What papers?* he wondered miserably. And they were plotting to kill his uncle. An instant before, he had wanted nothing more in the whole world than for Tom to come riding up. Now he desperately wanted his uncle to stay away! And who was Mullins? The only Mullins he knew was the fat, self-important storekeeper. Surely *he* couldn't be mixed up in this—why, he was one of the church leaders! Of course, he reminded himself, his father had never cared for the man; said he "gave himself airs."

These thoughts ran through Nathan's mind as the jolting ride resumed. The trail they followed became narrower and steeper until the ground over which Nathan hung suspended had dropped away two hundred feet below! Now Nathan tried to hold his breath on purpose for fear that even inhaling might overbalance him and send him plummeting into the depths of White River Canyon. He tried closing his eyes, but immediately felt dizzy and sick to his stomach and in danger of losing his precarious perch.

Yancey noticed his stiffened little body and remarked dryly, "Don't go to pukin' on me, boy, or I'll figger that this here canyon is a powerful good spot to drop ya inta!"

When the gorge finally bottomed out and widened as it neared the town of Tailholt, Yancey directed his horse down the remaining six feet of bank that separated the cliff face from the river bottom. The river was dry at this time of year, but would soon enough be an outlet for the rains to find their way downward into the San Joaquin Valley.

Yancey's gelding moved silently through the soft sand toward the farther bank. There a dense thicket of cottonwoods obscured the view of the river from riders on the Tailholt road. The bay stopped of his own accord as if they had done this maneuver before. Yancey cocked his head first one direction and then the other as he listened for travelers before crossing the road.

Nathan felt a surge of hope. They must be close to the town where there was a little hotel and a few businesses. Tailholt was a rough mining camp, but there were some good people there who would surely help him to escape from this killer. If only he could give some sign, let someone know! But there wasn't anyone around to hear if he yelled; and trussed up as he was, he couldn't hope to make a run for it.

A bellowing voice floating up toward their place of concealment froze Yancey's intended movement to urge his mount up the bank. Someone was coming up the road! As quickly as Nathan's spirits soared they were brought to earth again by the cold sharp pain of Yancey's knife pressing in behind his ear. In a threatening voice made all the more sinister by its hoarse whisper, Nathan heard Yancey murmur, "Not a peep, d'ya hear? I'd as soon stick ya as look at ya."

The bellowing voice grew louder, and then a creaking sound was heard, and an intermittent popping noise—a bullwhacker and his team of oxen.

"Curse your hides you ill-gotten sons of perdition. *Crack!* Can't ya move any faster? *Crack!* I'll sell ya for hides and tallow right where ya stand! *Crack!*"

This fountain of curses and whip-cracking noise

sounded as if it would pass by and go on up the hill, but all at once it stopped directly in front of Yancey and Nathan.

The drover could be heard exclaiming, "Well, how are ya, ya old horse thief?" This was apparently directed to someone whose approach down the road had been masked by the bullwhacker's carrying on.

Whoever the second party was, he was considerably more soft-spoken than the drover, and so only half the conversation could be heard. "Ya don't say? Up Havilah way? I thought that was all played out years ago."

There was a pause, then, "Not me, hoss, not me. Why, these four-legged devils are sure enough like stone, but at least they move when I tickle 'em! *Crack!* Show me the hard rock mine that'll do that, and I'll join ya."

The unseen and unheard second party to this conversation must have been riding a horse, for it chose this moment to nicker, and quite unexpectedly, Yancey's gelding answered it!

Yancey immediately leaned forward over its neck to silence it with a restraining hand, and the point of his knife pressed deeper into Nathan's flesh. The boy gasped, but remained still as a tiny trickle of blood began running down the side of his face and dripping off his nose. Both Yancey and Nathan held their breath— the one in fear of discovery, and the other in fear of death.

A moment more and both released quiet sighs, for from the road they heard, "Jim Dobber is dead? Ol' 'Mud' Dobber hisself? Why, I'da thought he was indestructible. Measles, ya say?"

At last the bullwhacker announced, "Well, ol' cuss, we'd best be movin'. I want to top the grade afore sundown. Go along, ya useless lumps! *Crack!* Rattle your hocks afore I cut out your brand marks an' sell ya for strays! *Crack!* Be seein' ya, ol' cuss!"

A short while later Yancey crept up to the edge of the cut and noted that the road was clear in both directions. Occasionally a shouted curse and the pop of the drover's whip could still be heard echoing down the canyon, but it was getting fainter and farther away.

"Ya done real good, boy. You was right smart to set so quiet. That loud-mouthed teamster may figger he can tickle his ox real clever with that fool whip, but jest you mind how good I can tickle with this little play-pretty of mine." So saying he drew the flat of his knife across Nathan's neck once more for good measure, and then they rode on across the road.

———————

Mont was just beginning to come around. His head hurt, and his bound wrists and ankles ached. Unlike Nathan, Mont had no idea where he was or where Byrd was taking him. He was smart enough to realize that any sudden movement or sound might get him clobbered again, so he remained still, pretending unconsciousness. Byrd had naturally chosen the easier side of the canyon for himself to travel, so Mont had awakened to the view of a gently sloping hillside below him, not the rocky gorge that Nathan was being forced to watch.

Mont was not aware of it, but their travel was following the road from Greenville to Tailholt, about two hundred yards off to one side. It seemed to him that they had been traveling forever; in fact, the afternoon was drawing to a chilly close when Byrd Guidett muttered "Whoa" to his big bay horse, and they stopped in the shadows of the ridge's northwestern fringes.

Below them was the gold-mining community of Tailholt. Its thousand or so inhabitants were already indoors, away from the wind that had an increasing bite to it. In some of the windows the glow of lanterns was beginning to appear. Mont looked wistfully toward the warm, snug little homes.

"Awake finally, eh?" grunted Byrd. "You ain't the only one wishin' to get inside by a fire and hunker down with some decent food." Then, as if even this brief observation had betrayed too much gentleness, he shoved Mont roughly off the horse onto the hard ground with a thud. "Wal', we ain't goin' to no nice warm cabin, see? An' if'n ya don't tell us what we want to know and that right quick, I might jest tie you up to a rock and see how soon some bear comes to make a meal off'n ya, if'n ya don't freeze to death first!"

Both man and boy were chilled and stiff by the time Yancey and Nathan rejoined them. Byrd was even grumpier than usual. "Whar ya been? You musta stopped for supper, and me afreezin' my rear off out here!"

Yancey for once was in no mood to be cowed by Byrd's menacing talk. "Get down off yer high horse, Byrd Guidett. You know'd we had to take the long pull around Tailholt, besides pickin' our way down that canyon. An' then I had to wait near an hour to cross the road. Some bullwhacker freightin' up to Keyesville met up with some'un comin' down, and they went to palaverin' right in front of me! An' what am I s'posed to do, ride on acrost sayin', 'Pardon me, boys, whilst I get to my hideout, an' pay no mind to this trussed-up brat here'?"

Even Byrd was taken aback by Yancey's tone. "They didn't see ya, then?"

" 'Course not! Now, are we gonna stay here shootin' off our mouths, or are we gonna get on up the trail?"

When they had ridden up into the hills some mile and a half, they came to a wide expanse of shale rock with no dirt covering. Carefully, they began picking their way across the dangerous surface until at last they rode off onto broken ground about a half mile from where they had last made a track. Yancey passed his reins to Byrd and slipped off his horse, leaving Nathan to balance across the gelding with even greater difficulty. As Byrd rode and led Yancey's mount, Yancey moved along behind, smoothing out the sign of their passing with a handful of brush. He did this for perhaps another four hundred yards until satisfied that even if someone were able to trace them as far as the shale, their path after that would be impossible to pick up.

Byrd paused long enough for Yancey to mount up again; then both men urged their horses upward at a good pace. Nathan thought with a shudder that they were now climbing up Shadow Ridge itself. Somewhere up on these lonely heights his father had died. He also knew that somewhere to the east awaited his home and his mother; but this cold, inhospitable and sinister mountain lay in between!

The way the cave appeared was startling. Even Byrd and Yancey, who had seen it many times, were amazed at the suddenness with which the opening seemed to be right underfoot, where there had previously been solid granite mountainside.

The western rim had grown increasingly steep and barren for the last hour of the ride, with no features to attract anyone's attention. No entrance of any kind was visible—no boulder-strewn lip, no telltale shadow. What existed was a slightly flattened area—no more than a bench on the slope, and so near the tip that it seemed too small to contain anything worth investigating. Just inside this flattened space was the mouth of hell, so it seemed. A gaping black hole, at first a vertical shaft, resolved itself into a sloping entryway down into the earth.

The level bench near the mountain's peak coincided with an outcropping of limestone. This slight declivity caught the runoff and snowmelt, which gradually melted away the limestone, leaving a near-perpendicular crater. Some time later an earthquake had collapsed a portion of the edge, and that occurrence, combined with still later landslides, had provided access to the depths.

Byrd's horse sniffed the air over the opening as if to say, "This looks familiar, but I'm still not sure I like it." Then he stepped downward into the granite rubble that formed the ramp.

Once down the short slanting heap of debris, the cave's entrance disappeared almost immediately under a granite roof. Just inside this roof the cavern made a sharp turn to the right so that even though the crater was exposed to sunlight, very little reached the interior of the cave past the first few feet.

Byrd reached out toward the wall and grasped a lantern that sat on a rocky ledge just level with a man on horseback. Fishing around in his shirt pocket for an instant, Byrd removed a match, which he struck on the rough wall and applied to the wick.

The warm yellow glow revealed a level floor of trampled gravel, and a crude barricade of branches that blocked the entrance from the first bend of the tunnel. There, just across the rude fence were two more horses, who whinnied a greeting to the two ridden by the outlaws. Interested in spite of his aching muscles and his fear, Nathan raised up for a look. The horses may not have been signalling to their equine counterparts, after all, but reacting to the presence of Mont and Nathan. Nathan recognized both animals as having been stolen from their ranch!

Byrd and Yancey stepped from their mounts, and Yancey pulled aside two rails of the barricade. They led their horses in among the other two, with the boys still hanging over the saddles. Once through the opening Yancey replaced the fence, and then Byrd yanked both children to the ground. With a pocketknife he slit the rope that tied their ankles, but left their hands bound. "Get up," he growled roughly, gesturing for the two to precede him deeper into the cave.

Yancey lit another lantern and began to unsaddle the horses as Byrd led Mont and Nathan over another fence at the rear of the cavern. The glow from his lamp pushed back the darkness just far enough for them to see that the room they were leaving was as large as a small barn and obviously well suited for that purpose. Along one side of the passage was a channel in the rock that was filled with water like a cistern. The pool of rainwater that had formed this cave was still present, but its location was now below the surface. As the tunnel narrowed and angled downward, the pool's overflow continued downward into the mountain, as it had for ages past, and formed the tunnel through which they walked.

Mont's feet had evidently been bound more tightly than Nathan's, for he was having difficulty walking. His stumble to the fence had been managed clumsily, and now, just on the other side of it, he fell.

"My feet!" he exclaimed. "They's all needles!"

"Get up and move, ya little varmint! Do ya think I'm gonna carry ya?" With that he grabbed Mont by the collar and jerked him to his feet. "Now walk!"

"Come on," encouraged Nathan, "lean against me. I'll help you." So saying, Mont stumbled next to Nathan, and then the two lurched down the passageway.

The cave had become both narrower and lower after exiting the room for the horses; now it opened out again into a space of room-sized proportions. Byrd lifted his lantern as they entered; they had evidently arrived at the gang's living quarters. A crudely constructed fire pit stood along one wall, the surface completely blackened with soot. Black streaks ran upward until they disappeared into the shadows of the craggy ceiling, where a crevice leading to the surface provided natural ventilation.

A pile of supplies, cans of beans, and a flour barrel were jumbled together in one corner, while a heap of empty cans and other rubbish made up a garbage dump in another. Along two walls were bed frames with wooden sides and cross-laced webbing made of leather. These meager belongings and a small table with two crude chairs standing in the center of the open place comprised the entire furnishings of the room.

On the wall opposite the way they had entered were two dark holes that showed as exits. Into one ran the underground stream that had passed through this cavern along one wall and which could be heard gurgling into the passage beyond. The other opening was some-what uphill from the rest of the cave—another stream of water had at one time flowed into this room, but it had since dried up.

Byrd gestured for the boys to sit down in the chairs, and he proceeded to light a fire in the fire pit, igniting some kindling that had been set there before. As this caught, he added small oak branches, and soon the air became noticeably warmer. He then scooped up a cof-feepot full of water from the stream and set it on a flat rock next to the blaze.

Yancey came in from tending the horses just as Byrd dumped a double-handful of ground coffee into the boil-ing water. He tossed a can of beans to Yancey, and both men deftly opened the tops with their knives and then used the knife blades to eat with. Byrd poured himself a cup of coffee and then poured one for Yancey. All this fixing and eating and pouring had been done without a single word being spoken and without any acknowledg-ment of the boys.

Nathan endured the smell of the beans and the aroma of the coffee as long as he could, then remarked timidly, "Please, may we have some food too?"

Byrd flung his now empty can onto the rubbish pile and towered menacingly over the boys. "You two are a hull mess o' trouble. Why, we got blasted little here as it is, an' not to be wasted on the likes of *you*." He raised his arm as if to strike Nathan for asking, but Yancey interrupted.

"Hold on, Byrd. 'Member, they gotta be able to talk here directly, so we'd best feed 'em some."

Byrd looked as if he begrudged them so much as one mouthful, but he opened one more can of beans and unceremoniously dumped the contents on the table. After cutting their hands free he remarked, "There it is. Now go ta eatin' an' don't waste one bean."

The boys scooped up the tiny supper and licked their fingers.

"Next I suppose you'll be wantin' milk to drink or some o' my coffee." As the two small friends looked up hopefully, Byrd concluded, "Well, ain't that jest too bad? Get on over an' lap up some water like the two scrawny curs you are."

Leaving one lighted lantern on the table, Byrd took the other in his meaty hand and growled at the boys to follow him. He led them over to the dry side passage. It was a space no bigger than a pantry, a shaft reaching upward and into the dark, out of reach of the lamplight. Thrusting them inside, he gave them a warning.

"Don't try to run off, see? Ya cain't get up the shaft, an' if'n I catch ya tryin', I'll give Yancey"—here he jerked his thumb over his shoulder—"a chance to go to carvin' on ya with his toad-sticker. Ya know, they say the Comanch can peel a man's hide like skinnin' a spud. Wal', Yance there will make ya *wish* them Injuns had you instead!" He left, taking the lantern with him and leaving the boys in total darkness and abject misery.

CHAPTER 14

It was late afternoon before Emily noticed that the boys had been gone longer than she expected. She had been busy all day, alternating farm chores with household cleaning and stops to visit Jed in his sickroom. He was comfortable enough, but his fever came and went, and Emily spent much of the day sponging his forehead with cool water and bringing him cups of tea with sugar when the chills were on him. Near sundown, he slept, and Emily sank into the rocking chair near the fire, exhausted.

"Where can Nathan and Mont be?" she mused. "It's getting cold outside, and I can't imagine that the lunch I packed would keep them from coming home for supper." The thought of supper reminded her that she had a pot of soup simmering in the kitchen, and so with a resigned sigh she rose and went to check on it.

Through the kitchen window she heard the sound of hoofbeats and looked out to see Tom ride into the yard on Duncan. His hat was pushed back on his head in a jaunty manner, and he was grinning as he pulled saddle and bridle from the horse and gave it a good-natured swat to turn it into the corral. He disappeared for a moment as he walked to the front door of the house and then, as she expected, she heard his knock and a shout, "Emily, it's me, Tom."

She called out, "Come on in, Tom," then returned to the front room to meet him.

"Emily," he began without preamble, "guess what? They paid me the whole amount in gold. And that cavalry officer they brought along to inspect the horses said"—he drew himself up in military fashion and puffed out his chest to support an imaginary load of medals—" 'Son, these are the finest mounts I've seen this side of the Mississippi. We'll take as many more as you can deliver—and just as soon as you can have them ready.' 'Yes, sir, Colonel,' I said, 'we'll sure have them for you.' Where are the boys? I want to tell them how good we did."

"The salt and pepper twins aren't back from playing yet. I shooed them out of the house because Jed has come down with the measles. He's been in bed all day and been running a fever, but he's asleep now and doing all right, I think."

"Measles, eh? Say, that can be pretty serious. Have you ever had them?"

"Yes, when I was just a little girl. Have you ever had measles?"

"Same with me, I guess. I must have had them about Jed's or maybe Nathan's age. I felt pretty rotten for a week or so and broke out with a terrific set of spots, but then I got over it pretty quick. How about the other two? Any sign of them catching it?"

"No, not so far, although three children over at the school have had it, so I'm almost positive these three have had an equal chance. Really, the reason I sent them off today was so I could get some work done while it stayed quiet for Jed to rest. Then, too, if they are going to be cooped up with measles, I thought it would be better for them to run off a little excitement first."

"Do we need to get a doctor?"

"I did talk to Doc Welles and he said Jed just needed rest and good food. He said kids seem to do all right as long as they keep warm and still and don't get pneumonia. He did say that it was a lot tougher on adults. But enough about measles; tell me more about your great horse trading!"

Tom paused as if gathering his thoughts before going on. Then he began in a halting voice and a more serious tone, "Emily, on the ride to Ford Tejon and back . . . well, on the trip, I had a chance to do some thinkin'."

"Yes, Tom—thinking about what?"

"Well, you know I feel responsible for you and the boys and all. I mean, not that I mind or anything, but, you know, I want to see you taken care of. Do you understand what I'm saying?"

"No, Tom, I'm not sure that I do."

Flustered, Tom began to speak, stopped, then finally tried again. "You see, since we made out so well with the horses, and since it looks like we got a steady market, with the money being good and all, I was just thinkin'. . ."

"What, Tom? What are you trying to say?"

Tom drew a deep breath and plunged ahead. "It's this way. What with this sale and the prospects of more to come, there's plenty of gold put by for you and the boys to go back to Missouri now. I mean, you could go back and buy you a place of your own. Pay cash for it, too. I should have known you wouldn't want to be moving back in with your folks and imposing on them. Well, now you don't have to. You can get you a nice house, and I can send back more money right along as I get more strings broke, and . . . why, Emily, whatever is the matter?"

Tom had stopped speaking when he finally noticed that Emily's expression had changed and she appeared ready to burst.

"Ooh, you, you *dunderhead*! Didn't I tell you before that this is my home now? I wouldn't want to go back to Missouri if I could go as the Queen of Sheba. Get a place of my own, indeed! I *have* a place of my own, Tom Dawson, and it's here, right here! And to think I thought you . . . you were—ooh!"

"What, Emily, you thought what?"

"Just never mind, Tom. There's some soup on the stove. Help yourself while I go check on Jed. Then you might go out and holler for the boys if you've still a mind to be *helpful*. It's getting dark and past suppertime."

Tom went out to the kitchen, shaking his head and muttering as he went. Who could understand women? Everything he'd said was perfectly reasonable, even carefully thought out, and look how she reacted! And what else could she have possibly thought he meant to discuss? Unless, unless . . .

Tom shook his head again. No, it wasn't possible. It couldn't be, could it? He decided that he needed a little fresh air to clear his head more than he needed a bowl of soup right then, so he went out through the kitchen door.

It was getting late. The sun was already below the top of the mountain, and the wind had a nip to it. Even though the night was clear and the daytime sun had all but melted the snow, winter was definitely stirring. It might even freeze. He began to call out, "Hey, Nathan! You, Mont! Suppertime!"

When there was no response, he started walking slowly northward toward the creek bottom where he knew the boys liked to play. When he reached the place, they weren't there. He called to them again, but still got no answer. Tom began to walk along the creek in the direction he thought their games might have taken them; then he thought better of it and decided to go back for his coat and a lantern.

Emily was just coming out from checking on Jed. "Did you find them?" she asked. "I heard you calling."

"No," he replied. "And it's getting dark and cold outside. I think I'll grab a light from the barn and walk up the creek a ways." At Emily's worried frown he added, "Don't get upset. They probably just were having such a fine time that they wandered farther away than they intended. But Nathan knows this valley real well. He can find his way back. I'll just go help them along a little."

Out in the tack room Tom put on a heavy fleece-lined coat and lit a lantern. He thought briefly about saddling a horse and riding out, but figured that tracking two small boys at night was better on foot.

Tom was pleased to find that when he returned to the creek bed with lamp in hand, he could immediately pick up their tracks in the sand. He followed them along the stream's course, lost them briefly where they had turned aside to look at something, then picked them up again a hundred yards farther on where they had rejoined the creek's path.

When Tom arrived at the juncture of Poso Creek and Sandy Creek, Tom again missed the trail where the boys had left the sand to strike out across the hillside, so he circled back until he found it. From the point at which they exited, he thought he could guess where they might have been headed. It was a large rock that stood part way up the hillside—a good "lookout post" for the upper end of the valley. Just the place two boys who were out exploring would want to visit. Tom himself had used it before to survey the countryside when he went deer hunting.

When he reached the spot, he could tell that Nathan and Mont had been there, but they were not there now; worse yet, they seemed to have milled around there a lot, without giving a clear indication of which direction they had taken next.

Tom was heading back downhill when he came upon the other sets of tracks. The boot prints of two men appeared both coming and going on the hillside, and the outward bound set was pressed deeper into the earth as if the men had been carrying something. Tom's heart began to race. How could he be sure? He couldn't bring this kind of news to Emily without proof. After all, he didn't even know for certain that Nathan and Mont had been near the men. He decided to recross the area one more time to see if he could locate anything definite, any clue to the boys' presence.

———————

"Didn't you find them?" Emily asked when Tom returned to the house. At his negative response, she cried, "But where can they be? You don't think that someone could have. . . ?" She stopped as a grieved look came over Tom's face. "Oh no, Tom, not Byrd Guidett! But you can't *know*! I mean, maybe you just haven't looked in the right place yet."

She stopped again and followed Tom's glance downward to his right palm outstretched in front of her; then she sank onto a bench, and with her face in her hands, began to sob.

In Tom's hand, glistening in the firelight, lay Nathan's Barlow knife, taken from the tree trunk that marked the spot where a day of fun had turned into a night of terror.

"Oh, Tom, what does it mean? Where are the boys? What could have happened to them?" gasped Emily. "Could they be lost, or was it . . . was it . . . a wild animal? But no, they'd get up a tree, wouldn't they? Oh, Tom, where can they be?"

"Take it easy, Emily. Here, sit down," instructed Tom, grasping her arms and moving her toward the rocking chair.

"Sit down? We've got to go out looking for them. Where's my other lantern and my shawl? Tom, you've got to ride to town for help! Why are you just standing there?"

Tom sighed heavily. "Now, Emily, you've got to get hold of yourself. I've got something to tell you, and it won't be easy."

"No, Tom, NO! You can't mean—"

"Emily, calm down! I don't think they're dead. In fact, I don't think they're even hurt. Do you recall that Byrd Guidett wanted to take Mont with him as some winnings in that poker game when he killed the man?"

"Why yes, of course. And you stopped him, and . . . oh, Tom, you don't think Byrd took him and Nathan!"

"Yes, I do think that's what happened, Emily. There were tracks of two men near where I found the knife, and some sign of a scuffle with the boys. I followed their trail to where they had tied their horses; then I came back here to tell you. Now, Emily, there wasn't any blood, nor any sign that the boys had been harmed. Byrd and that partner of his could have ki—hurt the boys right where they caught 'em if they'd intended to."

"But why take them away, Tom? What do they want?"

"I don't know the answer to that, Emily. Byrd may still be tryin' to get hold of Mont, but there must be more to it than that. Even the fight he and I had at the Bella Union didn't seem strictly due to Mont. It's more as if Byrd wants to get at me for something, or he thinks the boys know something . . . I don't know what . . ." His voice trailed off as he realized that he couldn't come up with anything helpful or encouraging to say.

"But he must know he'll be tracked, trailed where ever he goes, and brought to jail!"

"Yes, I'm sure he does. And that means two things."

"What, Tom, what?"

"He's not gonna leave a trail that's easy to follow, and whatever he thinks he can accomplish by taking the boys must be real important to him! Now, I'm riding to town to get help. You stay put and take care of Jed. I'll be back just as soon as I can."

———

The first person Tom called on when he arrived in Greenville was the Parson Swift. Even though awakened from a sound sleep, the parson came quickly to the door and admitted Tom to the parlor. As the minister listened attentively to Tom's story, Swift stoked up the fire in a small chrome and cast iron stove, his mind racing.

"Everything you say makes sense to me, Tom," he

concluded. "I think we need to rouse the town and get started right away. The longer we wait, the farther ahead they'll be, and the more chance for them to cover their tracks. Let's go over to the church."

So saying, he wrapped his robe tighter around him and retrieved a worn pair of carpet slippers from his bedroom. "I explained things to Mrs. Swift," he said as they went out the door. "She'll be brewing some hot coffee for us."

Over the entryway of the little church was a narrow steeple containing one high-pitched bell. Parson Swift grasped the bell rope firmly, and with strong sweeps of his wiry arms, he began pealing the alarm. Its clanging sounded unnaturally loud in the clear, crisp night air. Soon the interrupted silence was further broken by the sounds of dogs barking and horses neighing. A few moments later lights began appearing in windows, and exclamations and slamming doors echoed off the hills around the town

Deputy Pettibone, to his credit, was the first to arrive, his nightshirt hanging down over his trousers. In one hand he was carrying his boots, and slung over his other arm was his gun belt. "Where's the fire, Parson? Is the church burning, or what?"

"It's not a fire, Deputy, it's—" Before the Parson could complete his answer, the Volunteer Fire Company arrived, pulling their pump cart by hand. The water wagon arrived next, pulled by a team of snorting draft horses that looked far more alert than their driver, who sawed at the reins while alternately blinking, yawning and cursing.

"Come into the church, men, come in," called the parson, realizing that explanations would be futile until everyone was assembled and quiet. Confusion ruled as newcomers inquired, "What's this about, then? Ain't there a fire. No, it ain't, it's the livery stable. Naw, it's no fire atall; Jeff Davis has been captured!"

Pettibone stood up and raised his hands for silence. Gradually it grew quiet in the room, and the deputy addressed Parson Swift in a somewhat squeaky voice. "Just what's this here alarm about, Parson? Is there a fire or ain't there?

"Just quiet down, men, quiet down," instructed the preacher as the babble threatened to erupt again. "Yes, there is an emergency, and no, it's not a fire. Tom Dawson here will explain."

Quickly Tom outlined the situation—how long the boys had been gone, what he had found and where, the tracks he had followed, and what he thought it all meant. "So you can see we need to get after them right away. There's no telling what they'll do to those boys. Guidett's already shown how he treats folks in this town."

Mutters of agreement and a general movement out the door was halted by a measured voice raising carefully chosen phrases at the rear of the room. "May I suggest that we not be hasty, gentlemen? The night, while cold, is not desperately so, and the great likelihood is that the two children have merely wandered too far from home and have curled up somewhere for the night." Robert Mullins paused, then continued. "Most probably they've found some warm spot to get into, one of our neighbor's barns or haylofts, and are now peacefully sleeping—even as we all should be."

"Didn't you hear what I said, Mullins? I found my nephew's knife and the boot tracks of two men, even some sign of a struggle!" Tom Dawson burst out angrily.

The parson laid a restraining hand on his arm.

"Now, Mr. Dawson. Didn't you say that you discovered this 'evidence' after dark? How can you be certain what it means?"

"You gob of lard! I'm tellin' you my nephew and Mont James are in the clutches of that bloodthirsty killer *right now* and you want stand here jawing about proof?"

"Naturally, Mr. Dawson, your emotions are running rather high just now, and I think we all understand that, don't we, men? But let's not be hasty."

"Now jest hold on a minute there, Mullins," began stocky Bill Gardell. "If it was my kid, I'd be out lookin' right now, an' I'd want my neighbors to be helpin'."

"Just so, just so, Mr. Gardell. I wasn't suggesting that we not help. But if some sort of abduction has taken place as Mr. Dawson believes, don't we stand a much better chance of tracking them by daylight? In fact, if all of us went up there now, wouldn't we obscure the marks and actually make it more difficult to proceed? Let's seek expert counsel on this. Sheriff Pettibone, what do you think?"

"Well, I . . . I don't rightly know. I mean, those is little kids an' all. Still, tracking by night is hard enough, an' if we was to trample the ground, well then, where would we be?" Pettibone stopped as if not sure what point he'd just made. On that his audience was in complete agreement, but Robert Mullins covered the awkward silence just as if Pettibone had offered a masterful summation.

"Exactly right, Sheriff. And friends, may we remember one thing? The Dawson boy, assuredly one of our *own*, is accompanied by the young Negro child, no stranger to being a runaway, I assure you. Isn't it likely that under his influence, even a fine child like young Nathan could be led astray?"

Tom could contain himself no longer. "You mean because he's black, we needn't worry if he has disappeared or been stolen? He's no concern of ours? And some of that *taint* has rubbed off on Nathan, too? Is this what all of you believe? Mullins, you no good, lousy—"

"Now, Tom, no harsh words that you'd regret later," soothed the deputy. "I'm sure Mr. Mullins meant nothin' mean about either child. He was just tryin' to keep us calm. Tell you what, we'll all go out in the mornin', at first light. Now, what do you say to that?"

"I say I'm sorry I wasted my time comin' all the way over here to get help from my *neighbors*. Now get out of my way. Move over, I say, or I'll knock you down!" Tom shoved two men aside as he went up the aisle of the church and out the door.

"We'll join you at first light, Tom, you can count on us," called Pettibone after him. Several men looked ashamed, but no one except the parson moved to follow Tom out of the building.

Parson Swift laid a hand on Tom's shoulder just as he was about to mount Duncan. Tom whirled around, his right arm raised as if to strike.

"Oh, it's you, Parson," said Tom, dropping his fist. "Sorry, I—"

"You needn't explain, Tom. I'm as disgusted as you with the whole lot, especially Mullins and that spineless Pettibone." This was an astonishing comment since the soft-spoken preacher had never been heard to say a harsh word about anyone. "I'm not a woodsman nor any kind of a tracker, but if you'll have me, I'd like to go with you."

Tom stared at the parson for a moment, then

grasped his hand warmly. "Thank you, Reverend. If I don't burn this whole town to the ground, starting with Mullins' store, they'll have only you to thank. No, I'll go alone tonight. Come morning, some of these *neighbors* really might feel up to comin' to help, and they'll need someone to get 'em organized. Will you do that for me?"

"Of course I will, Tom, and I'll send my wife over to stay with Emily. I expect she's taking this pretty hard."

"You know she is. In fact, would you ask your wife to not say anything about this meeting to Emily? I'll just let her think there's folks who care in this town till maybe some of them wake up and find out they do!"

CHAPTER 15

At first light Tom stood again by the tree where he'd found the knife. He had little trouble picking up the tracks, though he frequently walked and led Duncan for fear of missing a turn. He reasoned that the two outlaws were carrying one child apiece, and that sooner or later they would hole up. He had to believe, had to hope that he was doing the right thing. He had no other alternative.

As Tom searched, he thought often of Emily—so brave but so grief-stricken. Would she be so insistent on making this land her home if she had seen the lack of concern among those she counted as friends? Could a return to war-torn Missouri have been any worse than this?

What was wrong with those people, anyway? Could they really abandon two children because they were afraid to get involved? Could the color of a child's skin mean that his fate was of no concern at all?

And what was Mullins' role in all this? As a merchant and a church leader, one would think that he'd be strong against any lawlessness and have a heart full of compassion. "Mullins' heart must be as cold as the coins in his cash drawer," Tom muttered. Now, what was it about Mullins' cash drawer that stuck in Tom's mind?

For some reason the image of Mullins standing over his counter stuck with Tom, but he couldn't for the life of him figure out why.

During the night another light snow had fallen on Shadow Ridge and the trail petered out completely. Try as he might, Tom could find no place where the two tracks had exited the snow field. Looking up the slope, with the morning sun behind him brightening the looming peak of the mountain, Tom could see no objective that any riders would have been trying to reach. There was no hideout, not even rocks big enough to conceal a horse. *They came up here purposely to lead me off*, thought Tom. *Then they backtracked their own trail, or rode down off this saddle somewhere and went toward Tailholt*. He was quite sure they would have avoided the main road only while it was light. Then when darkness had fallen, they could have returned to the highway. But how in the world could he figure out which direction or how far they had gone?

Turning his horse around, he wearily made his way back toward home. As he reached the place where he had begun to track, he came upon Parson Swift waiting for him. The parson looked expectantly at Tom, but said nothing. Tom shook his head sadly, and the two rode back to the Dawson place, where Emily and the parson's wife had kept an all-night vigil.

———

Mont and Nathan crouched together in their stony prison. They linked arms tightly not only out of fear but out of relief at finally, if only briefly, escaping the threatening knife point and punishing fists.

As their eyes adjusted to the light seeping from the larger cavern into their grotto, Mont could make out Nathan's tear-stained face. Nathan made no sound as he cried, but he couldn't hold back the tears any longer.

Mont listened for a moment to the noisy sounds of self-congratulations that issued from the other room, then decided he would risk a whisper. "Is you all right, Nathan?"

The hoarse, choked reply was unable to cover the lie even as Nathan spoke them. "I guess so. I'm okay."

"Is you hurt anywheres?"

Nathan's hand went up to the place behind his ear where Yancey's blade had been an inch from taking his life. "He cut me, Mont! He told me if I made a sound, I was dead! When we stopped by the road for that wagon to pass, he stuck his knife in my neck, and the blood ran down over my nose. I wanted to call out for help or jump down and run away, but I couldn't, I couldn't, you see!"

Nathan sounded close to sobs, so Mont made little hushing sounds and said, "Shh now, Nathan, we's still alive, and we's got each other."

"But I want to go home! I want my ma. What are they gonna do with us?"

"I don' rightly know what dey're fixin' to do wid us, but you know what my ol' mammie tol' me?"

"Your mama, Mont? I didn't think you remembered her."

"I dasn't talk 'bout her much, 'cause it makes me real sad, but I 'member she tol' me 'bout Massa Jesus allus takin' care of me. She say, 'Mont, Massa Jesus, He see ever' sparrow where dey go. He see 'em when dey in de nest an' He see 'em when de cat be afixin' to get 'em. I 'spects He can take care of a little blackbird like you.' "

"But what about the sparrow that the cat *does* get—what about that?"

"Den it goes up to heb'en an' fly free all de day long, I reckon. But you an' me, we'll tell Massa Jesus dat we ain't ready jes' yet. I has only jes' found out dat I is free right here. I means, dey may have catched us now, but I doesn't belong to nobody! Now we needs to pray an' den go to sleep."

For a minute when he first woke up, Nathan didn't know where he was. When he realized the predicament, he felt a moment's panic when he couldn't find Mont. In trying to find some comfort on the hard floor of the cave, they had managed to squirm past each other and were on opposite sides from where they had fallen asleep.

It was impossible to tell how long they had slept. Light was still coming in from the larger tunnel, and since no outside light reached to this depth, Nathan couldn't tell if he'd slept ten minutes or ten hours. He felt rested, though, and hungry again, so he guessed that it must be morning.

There were no sounds coming from the other room. Nathan lay very still and listened, but all he could hear was the sound of gurgling water as it made its way through the cavern beyond and plunged downward into the mountain.

Could they have been left alone? Was it possible that the outlaws had gone away? Nathan glanced over at Mont, decided against waking him, and crept slowly and cautiously over to the chamber entrance.

Quietly he lifted himself up from his huddled position and peeked around the corner. The fire in the pit was out, burned to a small pile of ashes. The two outlaws were still present, both of them asleep on the rough cots.

Nathan backed up into the smaller space. He bent down and shook his friend gently to wake him, while keeping his other hand ready to clasp over Mont's mouth to stifle any sound.

Mont awoke with a start, but didn't make any noise. His eyes opened wide, and he understood instantly when Nathan placed a finger across his lips and then gestured for Mont to follow him.

One step at a time, eyes darting back and forth from bed to bed, the two boys tiptoed out into the room. Their advance was painfully slow. It was all Nathan could do to not make a run for it. They stole past the rough table, across the open space near the upward passage, then stopped abruptly.

"You'uns wouldn't be thinkin' of runnin' away, now would ya?" a raspy voice behind them drawled.

Both boys whirled around. Yancey was sitting up on his bed eyeing them with amusement. Nathan shuddered as he noticed that Yancey already had his knife out in his hand.

"No, sir, we just needed to get a drink of water, an' we didn't want to wake you," offered Nathan.

" 'Peers to me you went the long way round to get to the crick over thar, but go on now, help yerselves." Then as the boys actually did go to the tiny stream to get a drink, Yancey added in a lower, sinister tone, "I'm right glad you wasn't asneakin' off, 'cause I mighta had to stop ya. That coulda been real unpleasant for somebody." With these words he flipped his knife, faster than they could see his wrist move, hurling the blade into the table leg.

The sudden *thok* awakened Byrd, who sat up with a start. Yancey continued speaking to the boys. "Now Byrd thar, he don't hardly wake for nothin', but me, I sleep like a rattlesnake. Do ya know how rattlesnakes sleep, boys?" When the children made no reply except to shudder, he went on. "They sleeps with one eye open, and when they strikes, they hits hard! Some'un 'most always dies."

Byrd sat rubbing his face and shaking his shaggy head. "Was they tryin' to sneak off?" he growled.

"Naw," replied Yancey. "They wouldn't even think of such a thing."

After the robbers had made coffee and fried some thick slices of bacon, they tossed a couple of biscuits to the boys. They were hard as rock, but nothing else was offered, and neither child had any desire to ask for more.

"When's that Mullins s'posed to get here?" Byrd asked.

"He cain't get here afore tonight. He won't know that we got hold o' these two till we don't show at the cabin at noon. He'll be along right smart after that," concluded Yancey dryly.

"An' what'er we s'posed to do with these two brats? Why don't we jest find out 'bout them papers now an' be done with it?"

"Go right on ahead," commented Yancey. "Long as ya don't fix it so's nobody else can ask more questions later."

"All right, Nigger!" Byrd faced Mont, sticking his nose near his.

"Where'd that master o' yours hide them papers?"

Mont gulped before answering. "What papers, suh? I don' know nothin' 'bout no papers."

A powerful backhand caught him on the side of the head and sent him sprawling to the floor.

"Ya see, Yancey, I tol' ya we'd have trouble with 'im. His memory ain't workin' too good, but I expect I can help 'im along some."

He dragged Mont back roughly into the chair and continued. "Now 'bout them papers, boy. Didn't ya see that colonel you was with hide somethin'?"

At the shake of Mont's tiny head, another cuff landed on his other ear and knocked him into the table. Nathan jumped from his seat, shouting, "You leave my friend alone! He doesn't know anything about any old papers! Stop hitting him!" Byrd turned to grab Nathan by the throat when a voice from the lower outlet of the cave commented, "Yes, you'd best stop hitting him for now, Byrd. You might succeed in killing him before I find out what I want to know, and that would not make me happy." It was Robert Mullins!

"Boss, how'd ya get here so soon? I mean, how'd ya know already that we had 'em?"

"Apparently you two incompetents not only succeeded in making off with one child too many, but you left enough marks that the Dawson child's uncle could follow you in the dark! It took all my persuasion to see to it that there wasn't a posse on your trail last night!"

"But, Mr. Mullins," Nathan blurted out, a shocked expression on his face, "what are you doing here?"

"I might well ask the same thing of you, young Master Dawson. But I think I'd be addressing the wrong person." He fixed his stare on Byrd.

"They was together. I mean, we didn't think it'd be smart—"

"Guidett, your problem is that you *never* think. At

least for once you didn't leave a gory corpse behind to mark your passing. If you had, I don't think even I could prevent the fools who inhabit that miserable little town from tearing this mountain apart with their bare hands until they caught you."

Here he turned to address Mont and Nathan again. "Which is not to say that anyone would ever find two very small corpses if they were hidden inside this mountain. Perhaps you can persuade your little friend there to tell us what we want to know. What ails you, boy? Can't you stand up straight?"

"I . . . I . . . don't know. I feel real strange all of a sudden," said Nathan in a shaky voice.

"Come, come, boy, you'll have to do better than that! Shall I let Mr. Guidett resume his intended action at the moment I arrived?"

"No, please. I feel better now, just a little woozy is all. But please, sir, let Mont alone. He don't know anything about any papers."

"Is that so, boy?"

"Yassuh. I din't see no papers, an' Colonel James, he din't tell me 'bout none, neither."

"Hmmm. All right. Suppose for a minute that I believe you. Why don't you tell me where you stopped the night before Colonel James's unfortunate death?"

"I don' rightly 'member de man's name, suh. But it were a fine house next to a riber. Kinda on a island-like."

"What's that, boy? You mean to say you stayed *with* someone? You weren't just camped?"

"Oh no, suh. Dere was even a fine barn for me to sleep in, an' dey give me a real nice supper."

"Jehoshaphat! Think, boy, think! What was the name?"

"Shall I see if'n I can jog his memory some?" offered Byrd, but Mullins waved him back impatiently with his fleshy hand.

"I'se real sorry, suh. I spects I din't hear no names. Dis house was by a riber on one side, like I tol' you, an' had a slough on de other. An' jes' 'cross o' dat slough dere was a big field, an' folks was acampin' dere fo' de night, but we—"

"Stop!" shouted Mullins. "That's Baker's house and his field. Listen carefully, boy. Did the man you saw there look like this." Mullins gave a brief description of Colonel Thomas Baker.

Mont's eyes brightened, "Yassuh, dat's de very man! Can we go home now?"

The storekeeper squinted his piglike eyes, and a most unpleasant expression crossed his face; then it passed, and his usual ingratiating smile returned. "No, I'm afraid that won't be possible just yet. You see, we have to recover something from that house that belongs to me, and just in case we have trouble locating it, I might want to ask you some more questions. You just stay here as our guests for a while and behave yourselves, and I'm sure you'll be treated all right. Won't they, Yancey?" A look went between the two men, but nothing was said.

"Guidett, you come with me. Take good care of our guests, Yancey. Even young Dawson may have some bargaining value." Mullins and Byrd exited down the tunnel up which the fat man had lately come.

CHAPTER 16

"How could they be so spiteful?" questioned Emily. "Those two little boys, out there alone, or worse. How can people be so small?"

"It isn't that they're altogether hateful, Emily," corrected Mrs. Swift gently. "You must remember that they're terribly afraid for their own families as well. Most of them have lost kinfolk in the war, and lots of people want to raise their families out here in peace, just like you. Now that peace is threatened. Byrd Guidett is just a big bully, shooting up the church like he did, but he has made these folks see violence up close, and most of them would rather shut their eyes or run away. Still, may God forgive them for not going out to search at least. I'm praying that God will put a terrible weight on them until they do what's right."

"Can't we track the riders any farther?" the parson asked Tom, who was seated with his head bowed in sorrow and exhaustion.

"No, Parson, the little dab of snow we got last night was just enough to hide the tracks. If we had more help, maybe we could comb the whole canyon down to below the snow line and pick up the trail again, but I just can't cover all that ground myself."

"Then, what will we do?" sobbed Emily again. "We

can't just leave Nathan and do nothing."

"I'll help you, Uncle Tom," suddenly voiced a pale, thin figure in a long nightshirt. Jed stood in the bedroom doorway looking weak but resolute.

"Bless you, Jed, but no, you get back to bed," Tom replied. "The best thing you can do is get your strength back and stay here and look after your ma."

"I'll go out with you, Tom," Parson Swift offered.

"All right, Parson. There's nothing else to do but try. Let me get some grub together and some bedrolls, and we'll go. Maybe we'll get lucky and run onto the trail easier than I expect."

"We can bring something with us more powerful than luck, Tom. God loves those boys—and you, Tom, Emily, and Jed. We need to hold on tight to our faith and expect God to lead, even when there isn't a trail we can see with our eyes."

There was a knock at the door. When Emily rose to answer it, she swayed, overcome by fatigue and worry. The parson's wife gently but firmly seated her again and went to the door instead.

Standing on the porch was McKenna, owner of the Bella Union. "Is Tom Dawson nae aboot?" he asked. Then seeing Tom in the room, he addressed him. "I was nae in town last night or I would have been with ye sooner. When I heard what had happened, I coom straightaway. These others here have coom on, too."

"What others?" inquired Tom, coming to the door and peering out.

Outside in the yard, bundled up in heavy coats and looking sheepish, was a group of riders. Among them were Bill Gardell, Red Burton, Bob Davis, and a few others. "Hello, Tom," began Gardell. "Me an' some o' the boys . . . well, we figgered we didn't do right by you last night, but we want to make amends."

"Tell him the whole truth, Bill," urged Red. "When we got home last night and told our wives what went on at that meetin', an' how Mullins talked us inta not doin' nothin', me and Bill an' Bob here got lambasted real good. We was in Alex's havin' coffee this mornin' and kinda comparin' bruises when Alex got the gist of what happened, an' he allowed as how he'd horsewhip us if we didn't get over here right smart. Ain't that the size of it, fellas?"

A chorus of "and how" and "you bet" chimed agreement, and Davis added, "Truth is, Tom, I didn't sleep too good last night anyways. I figger we let Byrd Guidett bully us jest far enough. An' as for Mullins and his slick talk, well, you see neither him nor Pettibone is here now. We figgered we couldn't wait on them to lead no more, so here we is. That is," he added respectfully, "if you'll still have us."

"You bet I'll have you! Parson and I have just been sitting here trying to figure out how we could cover four hundred square miles between the two of us. Come in, fellows, and fill up your canteens with hot coffee; we've got some hard cold riding to do."

They went out in pairs to scour the hillsides. They took a bearing on the approximate direction the tracks were heading when last seen, then fanned out in a half circle before riding down to the snow line, so as to give themselves the broadest possible chance to pick it up again.

It was late afternoon when Red Burton spotted the

deep tracks that emerged from the snow on the gentler slope of the canyon-side that led down toward Tailholt.

Three rifle shots fired in close succession brought Tom and the others riding over. "Look here, Tom," said Red. "These tracks is fresh, and they come out headin' in the right direction."

"But that's the track of only one horse. Where did his partner go?"

"We figger they split up at the head of the canyon, plannin' on meetin' up later," replied Red. "An' Bob here agrees it's likely this one was up to no good, or else why'd he be ridin' over here on the hill with a good road no more'n a quarter mile away?"

"All right. It makes sense to me. Part of us'll follow this trail, but the others need to keep working their way down the opposite side, just in case the second rider turned off another way. Parson, you and Bob and Red come with me; Alex, if you don't mind, I'd like you to lead the other group."

"Whatever ye say, Tom. Coom on then, boys, we're nae followin' naught by sittin' here."

Tom's group followed the hoof prints down toward Tailholt without difficulty. They found where the rider had apparently waited for some time, and saw marks on the ground to indicate that something had been thrown there. Another set of tracks rejoined there, but Tom decided not to call the other group immediately, thinking they might come across some clue that would be helpful. He did send Bob and Red into Tailholt to ask if anyone had recently seen Byrd Guidett or two small boys. By the time they returned with negative answers to both questions, Alex's group had completed their search and joined up again.

"They didn't leave the boys anywhere along the trail, and no one's seen them in Tailholt. Let's figure that they went on from here and we'll follow this track up Shadow Ridge."

———

"They've hoodwinked us for sure," said Bob Gardell. "They rode up on this shale, then doubled back, dustin' their tracks as they went. Shucks, if they come this far in daylight, they could've chanced goin' back on the road by night an' be most anywheres by now."

Tom rose in his stirrups and looked anxiously up the mountain. "What about farther up? Couldn't they have crossed the slide rock and gone on up?"

"Naw, you can see for yourself there ain't nothin' up there," remarked Red. "Why, even a squirrel would stand out, no more brush than there is up there. Besides, what'd they do up there anyway but come back down?"

McKenna turned to Tom in apology. "I ken he's right, Tom. We're wastin' time on a cold trail."

"Are you all for giving up, then?" asked Tom quietly.

"Nay, nay, dinna misunderstand. Let's split up again. Some will ride through Tailholt an' doon the mountain, inquirin' of all travelers if they've seen aught of two men and two young lads, and others to do likewise up yon Jack Ranch way. Never ye fear, they canna stay hid for long."

Tom looked down at his saddle horn for a long moment before nodding slowly in agreement to this plan. All the riders turned their mounts then, making their way back down the hillside in single file. Tom was the last to leave. He turned his horse around, then turned in his saddle to look up at the bleak summit of Shadow

Ridge. He raised a clenched fist toward it in anguished helplessness. Something close to hatred was in his eyes as he turned again to follow the others.

———

It was five days before Byrd returned to the cave. When he did he was in a foul mood, and Yancey as well as the two boys shrank back from him.

"Five days hidin' out in that stinkin' swamp in a cold camp. Not even coffee, that fat pig says, we don't want to give away our presence."

"What about them papers?"

"Who knows? We ain't even got inside the house yet."

"Why not? Don't them folks ever leave?"

"Naw, it's worse than that. He's got a mess of Yankee officers stayin' with 'im!"

"Yankees! What we s'posed to do now?"

"Mullins went on back to his store—his nice, warm, dry store, an' left me to watch. 'Wait till day after tomorrow,' he says. 'If you haven't gained entry by then, go back and trade places with Yancey,' he says. 'I'd stay myself but my continued absence would be noticed.' That lousy, stinkin'—"

"What's the matter with him?" Byrd continued, indicating Nathan.

"Don't know exactly. He's been acting real poorly since right after you left. First I thought he was fakin', but I felt of him an' he's got the fever all right. Says his head hurts an' his throat, and he's breakin' out in some rash or somethin'."

"Well, I ain't gonna wet nurse no sick kid. Be just

too bad if he hauls off'n dies, now wouldn't it? Save us the trouble."

"No! No! Home! Mama, Mama, Mama! Jed, look out . . ." Nathan's voice trailed off, but he continued to thrash around.

"Listen here, boy, you'd best keep yer friend quiet. I'm gettin' powerful tired of his carryin' on," ordered Byrd ominously.

"Yassuh," replied Mont. "But he's burnin' up wid de feber, an' now dem spots is 'most all over his body."

"Yeah, well, give him some more water, but keep him quiet!"

"Yassuh." Mont tried to get Nathan's attention, but to no avail. Mont took off his own jacket and used it for an extra cover over Nathan's trembling limbs. He moistened his pocket handkerchief and used it to cool Nathan's fevered face.

Nathan continued to shiver all over as if he were in a freezing snowstorm without a stitch of clothing on. Mont looked anxiously at his friend, and then, making up his mind, got all his courage together and went into the larger room to address Byrd.

"Mistuh Byrd?"

"What is it now, Nigger?"

"My frien', he need to be next de fire, an' he need some hot food."

"Why ya little . . . I'll . . ."

"If'n he dies, Mistuh Mullins gonna be powerful upset. You'd best stop an' think on dat!"

Surprised that such a small person could stand up to him so forcefully, Byrd laughed. "All right, then, fix him a place by the fire, an' let's see if ya can cook. I'm almighty tired of my own cookin', anyways."

Almost as soon as Mont assisted Nathan to stretch out by the fire, the sick boy began to calm down. His contorted muscles relaxed, and he ceased muttering to himself and fell into a peaceful sleep.

Mont used this break in his constant attention to his friend to fill the cleanest pot he could find with fresh water from the stream and put it on a hook over the fire. As it began to heat, he got grudging permission from Byrd to use a small pocketknife. With it he shaved pieces of jerky into small bits, which he dropped into the pot.

Byrd dipped himself a cupful of this soup just as soon as it began to boil, but Mont continued to heat and stir the mixture until it had reduced to about a third of its original volume.

Nathan began to show signs of awakening as Mont poured out a small amount into an empty tin can to cool. As Nathan's eyes opened and he looked around the room, Mont aided him in sitting up halfway, and then held the can to his lips. At first Nathan sipped slowly, but little by little he ate more eagerly until he had consumed all that remained in the pot. He smiled gratefully up at his friend, then lay down and returned to a relaxed sleep.

———

"Nothin'—not a blessed sign of 'em!" reported Red. "Me an' Bob went clean to Tulare. We met up with drovers, an army patrol and even a band of Tuolomnes. None of 'em have seen Byrd, or two men with two kids, or even one black kid, for that matter. You have any luck?"

"Yeah, tons of luck, an' all of it bad," said Bill Gardell. "McKenna an' me went to Jack Ranch, Sugarloaf, even busted our hump gettin' over Portagee Pass, an' nothin' to see nor nothin' to hear about. It's like they dropped off the world. One thing's certain, though, Byrd must be mixed up in this, else it's right queer of him to disappear at the same time as those two kids."

"Where's Tom and the parson?" asked Bob.

"Parson went back to check on Mrs. Dawson an' give 'em the report, such as it is."

"And Tom?"

Bill and the Scotsman exchanged rueful glances. "We couldna get him to coom back with us and rest a spell," said McKenna. "When we could nae mair ride nor walk, he made us give him the rest o' our kit, and he rode out Howling Gulch way."

"Howling Gulch? That windswept hellhole? There ain't even water nor wood for fires up that rock-choked gully. What'd he think to find up thar?"

"Do ye nae ken, mon? Tom is near crazed with grief, and what's mair, he canna think on what will coom to Miss Emily if he canna find her lad."

"It's sure enough true what Alex here says," added Bill. "He's aclutchin' at straws."

Tom rode Duncan around a pile of rubble that had fallen from the heights of the narrow gorge into its narrow throat. The boulders and gravel completely filled the canyon to a reach of twenty feet up the walls. For the third time in the past hour Tom had to dismount from Duncan and look for a way to scramble around a dusty obstacle.

The sides of the gully were treeless, even brushless, in their barren disarray. It appeared to Tom that the only thing growing there was a fine crop of decomposed granite that flowed down the walls as if determined to prevent even the tiniest plants from ever taking root. The bottom of the canyon was dry, a stranger to any regular flow of water, though it showed the unmistakable marks of flash flooding. The gorge was a tremendous runoff channel when the storm clouds broke over the heights of Sunday Peak, but the swift passage of water did no more than aid the crumbling rock avalanches in keeping the sides scoured clean.

But it was neither the sliding gravel flows, nor the boulder-strewn gully, nor the violent passage of a temporary river that gave the canyon its name. Howling Gulch took its designation from the fact that the tiniest gust of wind reverberated down the plummeting walls, shrieking in exit at the canyon's mouth like demons being cast into everlasting torment. And the wind blew all the time.

It was blowing particularly hard today. A week of fruitless searching had brought Tom to the point of being alone in the search, and the rising volume of the canyon's howling heralded the approach of another wintry storm that had mercifully held off through much of the search for the boys.

Gravel blew into Tom's face, assaulting his eyes like red-hot sparks from the blacksmith's forge. He ducked his head down to his chest, and soon found that he could not lead Duncan and hold on to his hat with the other hand and keep his balance all at the same time. Leaving the horse to stand ground-tied for a moment, Tom made several attempts to fasten his bandanna over his hat's crown before he finally succeeded in bringing the ends together under his chin.

When he could next clear his vision, Tom looked upward at the rock slide he was trying to lead Duncan around. This pile of rocks seemed even more jagged, heaped up higher and the canyon sides even steeper than those he had crossed to get to this point. Tom considered trying to retrace his steps to the bottom of the gorge and try the other wall, but momentary glimpses across the rubble showed no more promise than what he was already facing. "I guess this is as far as you go, boy," he commented to Duncan. Tom retrieved a rifle from its scabbard on the horse and thrust a box of cartridges into the pocket of his heavy coat. He loosened Duncan's girth, but left the saddle in place. He was glad Duncan could be trusted to remain ground-tethered, for there wasn't anything he could be tied to, anyway. "Be seein' you," Tom remarked, to which the horse only made answer by turning about and placing his broad rump into the wind. *Fine send-off*, thought Tom with grim humor. *Even the horse turns his back on me.*

He struggled upward for the next twenty minutes before reaching the top of the rock dam. He was right to have left the horse behind, he reasoned, or he would not have made it this far at all. The wind was really howling now, a blast so fierce that Tom could not stand erect for fear of being blown back down the slope he had just climbed. The screech noise increased, sounding like a steam boiler about to explode.

Tom stumbled down the other side, heedless of the path he took—anything to get off the exposed ledge where he felt like a fly in the path of a descending fly swatter. Halfway down, his feet went out from under him on a patch of loose gravel. As his boots shot forward with increasing speed, Tom flung his arms out to the sides, grasping for anything that might offer a grip to stop his plunge. The rifle, flung against a quartz ledge to Tom's right went off on impact, but its roar was completely masked by the wind.

Tom fell heavily on his side against a boulder; the ribs broken in the fight with Byrd cracked painfully. This time it felt as if an even greater fist had slammed into Tom's body, and his breath was expelled in an agonized "Ooof!" Tom lay still, panting, trying to draw air back into his lungs.

He looked around in a daze, unable to see the rifle from where he lay, and anxious to locate it—not because of its firepower, but simply because he felt that he would have to have it to lean on if he were to stand up. For the moment he had completely forgotten why he came to be in such a place. As he crawled up the side of the rock against which he had fallen, each breath was like a spike driven into his side. His face was raw and bleeding from the gravel driven into it by the force of the gale. His hands were stiff and aching, and when he looked to see why, he saw that on one hand three fingernails had been ripped out by his scramble to find a hold on the rock face. The palm of the other hand was bloody with fingernail marks where he had clenched his fist in the agony of bruising his ribs.

"God!" he cried, "what am I doing out here? Why don't you help me?"

CHAPTER 17

"We is climbin' Jacob's ladder, we is climbin' Jacob's ladder, we is climbin' Jacob's ladder, sol'jers of de cross," sang Mont to Nathan. The two were sitting in the small cave where they had been sent by Byrd while he went to feed the horses.

"An' don't even poke yer noses out till I get back an' tell ya to, un'erstan'?"

So the two sat in the dark, and Mont sang softly, much to the delight of his friend.

"Mont, how long have we been here, anyway?" asked Nathan.

"I don' rightly know" was the reply. "An' when you was mos' outta your head wid de feber, dem days did drag on so. Bes' I can figger, we done been here 'most ten days since we was catched."

"Do you think they'll ever let us go, or is anyone ever gonna find us?"

"Shore we's gonna get outta here, you jes' wait'n see!"

They heard noises coming from the other cavern, but thought only that it was Byrd returning from feeding. There was a shuffling sound, a pause, and then another shuffling noise. It sounded as if some heavy sack was being dragged across the floor of the tunnel. Mont stopped singing so they could listen, but neither boy made any move to go see what it was.

Presently they heard a flop as if that same imagined sack had been carelessly thrown onto one of the cots. A long, drawn-out groan followed, then silence.

Their heightened senses anticipated Byrd's return from the upper tunnel even before they heard him enter the adjoining cave. When he did enter, they heard him say, "Yancey! When in thunder did you come? What ails ya, anyway?"

A hoarse croak that in no way resembled Yancey's voice replied, "It's the fever an' the pox. I'm like to die with it, Byrd. I couldn't watch no more, so I come up."

The boys heard and understood the clumping foot-steps that followed this announcement. It was Byrd backing up rapidly away from Yancey's bed.

"Well, ain't this fine! How're we s'posed to watch them kids an' Baker's if ye're alayin' here sick?"

"I'm cold clean through, Byrd Guidett, an' I ain't been dry since I left here. I can still watch them brats. You get on out to Baker's an' leave me be!"

"All right, all right, jest don't let them two put nothin' over on ya."

Some time later there was no sound from the other room, and no one had come to tell the boys that they could come out, or when it was time to eat. So they went silently to the juncture of the two passages and peered carefully around the corner. Yancey lay on his bed, breathing heavily. His hair hung in matted streaks across his face, and one arm trailed limply to the floor. Mont and Nathan looked at each other, and each knew what the other was thinking. Remembering how quickly Yancey had awakened on their last escape attempt, the boys decided to test him. Nathan called out softly, "Mister Yancey, is it time for supper?"

To their great disappointment, Yancey sat up immediately and regarded them with sunken, red-rimmed, bloodshot eyes. He stared at them, saying nothing and swaying slightly back and forth. "You two—" he began, but got no further as a racking cough shook his whole frame, bending him almost in two with the spasm of it. When he could speak again, it was to gasp, "You two get back an' keep still. Leave me alone!"

———

How long Tom had been lying stretched out across the rocky ledge, he didn't know. What finally roused him from his stupor was no new pain or another moment of violent activity. Instead, his conscious mind struggled to awareness because of a lessening of the storm's frenzy, a gradual slackening of its voice.

Tom took stock of his injuries before trying to move. His hands were stiff but no longer bleeding. All his fingers worked, though unwillingly. His face felt burned as if polished by the wind, but his vision was clear and undamaged. As for his side, he drew a cautious breath and was almost surprised that no sharp pain resulted. He sat up carefully and noted with gratitude that his rifle lay where it had landed—just on the other side of the rock on which he was lying. He turned his gaze around to look at the gravel pile on which he had fallen in order to begin calculating a path around it, but it was not the marks his boot heels had made that drew his horrified attention. At the point where his side had been crushed up against the rock, at the precise location where his next step would have taken him, there was an abrupt drop-off that fell straight down into the gorge. Leaning out, Tom could just barely see the bottom some hundred feet below.

He crept on forearms and knees over to the rifle. It was undamaged. Tom used it to pull himself upright, where he stood, shakily surveying the canyon. "God," he said aloud, "you are here with me. You were helping me even when I thought you'd left me all alone. Wherever Nathan and Mont are right now, won't you hold on to their hands like you did mine? And Emily too, Lord. Help her see that you know all about lookin' for lost children."

When Tom had struggled painfully back to where he had left Duncan, he found the horse patiently waiting. Taking a canteen from his saddle, he drank a swallow, then poured some water into his hat for the grateful beast. With another handful he bathed his face, then he took another long swallow. "Let's go home," he said to Duncan.

———

Not until late the next evening were Tom and Duncan able to get all the way back down to the area of Greenville. Though exhausted and sore, Tom felt an unexplainable calm.

When he arrived back at the Dawson ranch, he was received with exclamations of joy and made to sit next to the fire while Emily tenderly bathed his face and hands and put ointment on the deep scrapes.

Tom listened as she related to him that all the other searchers had again reported in, with no greater success than when Tom had last seen them. In turn, he told her what he had experienced. He didn't try to conceal his disappointment at not being able to locate Nathan nor the extent of his anger and frustration that had driven him up Howling Gulch.

"But, Emily," he added, "something happened to me up there. I haven't found the boys yet, but I know we're going to. And this isn't just false hope to make you feel better. I really believe God promised me he'd bring them home if I'd just trust Him."

"I know, Tom," she responded. "I've been praying for your safe return, and look what God brought you back from. Everyone has been here praying for you and the boys, especially Victoria Burton. She stayed with me all night last night."

"God bless 'em," he replied. "Now I just need some sleep; then I can go out lookin' again."

She brushed her lips against his. "I know you will, Tom, and God will be leading you every moment."

Back in his room, Tom fell instantly into a deep sleep. He awakened once to drink a small bit of soup, then slept again clear into the next night.

Tom was having a confused dream. In it he was trying to swim up a rockslide. He heard a shot and then a shout. It was his brother's voice. No, it was Nathan's high treble. Something was pulling him down. The air was thick like mud as he tried to come to the surface of Shadow Ridge, but the syrupy air didn't slow the rocks and boulders that went bounding past him—each one narrowly missing his head. Another shot and another shout. What was holding him back? He squirmed around to see. It was a silver chain, its links twined around his legs. The links glinted dully in a shadowy afternoon light. The chain wound around his boot tops and tightened around the cuffs of his trousers, the end of the chain dropping off down the hill. Someone was tugging on it, but Tom couldn't see who. Then came a shot followed by an agonized shout!

Tom sat bolt upright, covered with sweat. He rubbed his hand over his face and shook his head. What a nightmare! He had relived his brother's death, but with himself as the intended victim, and the unknown fate of his nephew thrown in as well. How vivid that gunshot, how lifelike the scream—

Tom stopped himself in mid-thought. Deliberately he forced himself to reexamine the confused scenes. What was it that bothered him so about the two sounds which were so deeply implanted in his consciousness? Tom forced his mind to return to the actual scene on the mountainside that tragic afternoon, comparing its events to his dream.

There was no sudden flash, no leap to an instantaneous understanding, but rather a gradual realization. Tom thought it through carefully, tested his conclusion, found it sound. He remarked out loud to himself, "The shot came before the shout. That means that Jesse's gun didn't go off in the fall; he was shooting at something before he was struck. Something, or *someone*."

"If that's true," he reasoned, "then somebody wanted his death to *look* like an accident. They wanted to keep us from finding something, but they didn't want to let on that there was anything anybody would want to find."

He debated whether he should wait until morning to tell Emily, but he couldn't sleep, so he dressed quickly, deciding that he would walk around a little and think.

When he got outside his room, he noticed a thin sliver of light coming from under the window shade in

Emily's room. Perhaps she was still awake. He went to the front door and tapped gently, not wanting to disturb her, yet willing her to be awake. His quiet knock was rewarded with a shuffling noise followed by a gentle "What is it?"

"Emily," he called, "can I come in and talk a minute? I think I've figured something out."

"Of course, Tom. Just a moment."

He waited as she drew back the bolt and stepped aside to let him enter. Her hair was down on her shoulders, and she was wearing a dark blue dressing gown. She didn't appear to have just awakened, but Tom asked, "Did I wake you?"

"No," was the reply. "I couldn't sleep, so I was up reading the Ninety-first Psalm and praying for Nathan and Mont. What's this you've figured out?" she asked eagerly. "Do you know something of the boys' whereabouts?"

"Maybe. Maybe," he said slowly as this new aspect of his dream entered his mind. "Listen to me. I'm sorry," he said awkwardly. "Can we sit down?"

"Come into the kitchen, Tom, and I'll make us each a cup of tea."

While he sat at the kitchen work table, she stirred up the wood stove with a few pieces of oak wood, then put on the kettle. She sat down across from him and looked expectantly at him.

"Now, this may be nothing at all, so don't get your hopes up," Tom cautioned, "but the dream I had . . . I think it means something."

"Tell me from the beginning, as much as you can remember, and don't try to explain it till you're all done," she instructed.

His dream, which had seemed to last for hours at the time he had had it, took only moments to tell. He went slowly and carefully, trying to recall every event, every sight, and every feeling. "You see, it was the order of the two noises that bothered me up there that same night on the mountain, but I was too dazed to figure out what it meant. Later on, there was you and the boys to see to, and I guess I sort of blocked it out, just not wanting to think about it. But now," he resumed firmly, "I'm certain that what I heard was Jesse getting off a shot at whoever was pushing the rocks off the rim at him, and the shout just before the—" He stopped, unwilling to cause her more pain.

But Emily was all business now, the mother bear scenting the air for danger and preparing to defend her cubs. "Yes, I see. Whoever killed Jesse did so in order to prevent you two from either finding a route over, or discovering some secret about Shadow Ridge, *without* causing further investigation. That must mean," she continued, "that you and Jesse were right about the stage robberies and Byrd Guidett being linked with a hidden way to cross. And perhaps," she concluded, "it may mean that Nathan and Mont are being held there now!"

"At the very least," Tom pondered aloud, "there may be a clue to their whereabouts up there. And I aim to find it." He made as if to rise, but Emily stopped him. "Wait," she said, "there was more to the dream; let's not run off without working it all out while it's still fresh in your mind." The kettle was whistling on the stove, and Emily poured its contents into her blue china teapot.

"But it was all so confused and tangled," Tom protested. "How can it help us any?"

"Tell me the last part again," she urged. "About the chain."

"It was a silver chain that led down into a dark hole, and someone I couldn't see was trying to drag me backward into the path of the rockslide. It was all wrapped around my legs. I remember especially that the links were around my cuffs, heavy silver links twisted around my cuffs, and—"

"What, Tom, what is it?" Emily asked as Tom got a faraway look in his eyes.

"Cuffs and links, Emily—cuff links! I'm sure that's it! Now I know why Mullins didn't want anyone to go up Shadow Ridge, or to get a posse to chase after Byrd."

"Wait, Tom, you're not making any sense. What cuff links? And do you mean Robert Mullins, the storekeeper? What about him?"

"Pour us some tea, Emily, while I explain," Tom said confidently. "I even know now how we can check to see if I'm right."

CHAPTER 18

A solitary dog barked in sudden alarm, and Tom froze in his tracks. He listened intently, every sense tuned for the banging door or creaking hinge that would indicate someone coming to investigate. Two anxious minutes passed with Tom pressed against the side of the hardware store; then the dog lapsed into silence, apparently satisfied that he had successfully repelled the intruder.

When another minute's silence went unbroken, Tom breathed a sigh and resumed creeping toward the store's rear door. He was struggling not only with the worry of being caught but also with how he could explain his actions. He doubted that anyone other than Emily would put as much credence in his dream as he did. Even in the midst of this exploit, which Tom felt driven to perform, perfectly reasonable objections kept asserting themselves. How could a man of such recognized standing in the community as Robert Mullins be a party to the crimes of murder and kidnapping? Could such a pompous but ingratiating manner conceal such sinister intentions? Tom's agony at uncovering the fate of his nephew and Mont drove him to believe the answer was yes; not only was Robert Mullins a mass of flesh but a heap of duplicity as well.

And that, Tom reasoned, *is why I can't go to Pettibone or any one else with this suspicion without something to back it up. Even if I could convince them to investigate, I might only succeed in giving Mullins enough warning to get away or cover his tracks some other way.*

So here he was, on a bitterly cold and thankfully dark night, preparing to break into Mullins' store. He knew what he was seeking, but even Tom wasn't sure why. He intended to retrieve the silver cuff link that had come from the body of the man slain by Bryd Guidett. For some reason Mullins had chosen to appropriate the cuff link and squelch any further reference to it. Tom's gut feeling told him the cuff link had some bearing on the whole mystery.

Tom wore his Colt Navy strapped to his side. He didn't expect to be using it tonight, but he wouldn't have felt safe without it. Tom wasn't certain how he intended to enter the store. He had chosen the rear because the front bordered the two mains avenues of travel through the little town and made discovery much more likely.

Tom located the outline of the door and began to explore it with his hands. A quick investigation of the frame left Tom completely disgusted with himself for coming out on such a fool's errand without having found some pretext to check out this entrance first. His rapidly numbing fingers found that the rear door was completely set into the frame. It closed from the inside only and was apparently bolted from within, leaving neither bolt nor hinge on the outside. There was no lock to be broken, and the fit was so tight that there was little chance that a prying tool would work.

Now what? Tom wondered. *I've come this far; I'd best not go back without checking for some other way in.*

He circled the store cautiously, checking all the windows on the off chance that one had been left ajar. No such luck. He had almost reached the front of the building when he heard a noise from the road. No dog this time. Instead, it was a steady, measured footfall. Tom crouched down at the corner behind a scrawny lilac bush just off the porch that ran across the front. He hoped he would blend into the other dark shadows and not be noticed. The footsteps turned off the gravel of the roadway and went unhesitatingly across the small yard with its two hitching rails. The unknown person stomped heavily up the wooden steps to the porch and paused in front of the door. The jangling sound of a ring of keys came to Tom's ears, and he realized with a start that the bulky figure was Robert Mullins himself.

Tom's mind whirled at this complication. Should he wait until the shopkeeper had entered, and then make his own getaway? Should he step up and boldly confront the man, hoping that the shock of his unexpected presence would surprise Mullins into revealing something? The hesitation caused by these two conflicting plans settled the issue for him, for as Mullins located the correct key and proceeded to unlock the door, he began to mumble aloud. Tom leaned forward to catch what was said.

"Should have thought of this before. Can't depend on that rattle-brain and his shifty-eyed sidekick . . . Think of some pretext to get into Baker's . . . Delivering something . . . Show him the recognition tokens. Ha! We can . . ." His words trailed off into inaudibility as he snapped the bolt back and threw open the door. He closed it behind him but did not latch it on the inside.

Casting aside most of his caution, Tom moved quickly up onto the porch. He pushed the door open just slightly, hoping to hear more of the monologue without alerting Mullins. Tom peered carefully into the store through a window just beside the entrance.

At first he couldn't make out anything inside; then a spark of light flared as Mullins struck a match and lit an oil lamp on his counter. The hulking form fumbled with the key ring again before selecting another one with which to unlock his cash drawer. Suddenly Mullins threw the ring of keys down on the counter. "Can't get too excited," he murmured. "Know they're in the safe where they belong. Can't be too careful. Oh, but we're close." He turned his massive body around with some difficulty in the narrow space behind the counter and made a wheezing sound as he bent over to reach his safe.

Silently praying that the hinges were well oiled, Tom eased the door open and slipped inside. He tiptoed almost up to the counter. From behind it a mixture of grunting noises and the soft click of the combination lock could be heard. On the wall an ugly shadow-beast— half pig and half bear—played and stretched. A final click and the clank of the handle, and then Mullins gave a snort of satisfaction. He tossed something over his shoulder to the counter. No, it was *two* something: a pair of silver cuff links like the one bearing the initials J.D.!

Robert Mullins rose ponderously to his feet with the lamp in one hand and turned around to find himself looking into the cold, murderous gaze of Tom Dawson.

"Why, Mr. Dawson!" sputtered Mullins, "whatever are you doing here at this time of night?" Then, as if he realized that was not the proper tone to use, he added, "I'll thank you to leave my establishment immediately. If you have business to transact or something to discuss, come back tomorrow."

When Tom said nothing but continued staring into Mullins' startled and apprehensive eyes, the shopkeeper struggled to regain his composure. He put the lamp down on the counter. "I mean to say, why are you sneaking in here like this? Is something wrong? Is there an emergency?" His hands, like two fat spiders, began crawling across the counter top toward the cuff links.

At last Tom spoke. "Leave 'em right there, Mullins. I wouldn't want one of 'em to disappear before Colonel Mason had a chance to ask you how you came to be in possession of the twin to the cuff link found on a corpse!"

"Why, I can't think how it came to be here. I mean, I was looking for something else when—"

"It won't wash, Mullins. I heard what you were mumbling about recognition tokens. Let me take a guess. J.D. wouldn't stand for Jeff Davis, would it? Now, unless you want me to partly settle accounts with you about my brother before I turn you over to the army, you'd better tell me quick where the boys are."

A crafty smile played across Mullins' features. "Well now, that is the problem, isn't it? If you want to see your nephew safe, I suggest that you let me go. You understand the character of the two men who are holding them, don't you? If I'm not able to call them off, well, let's just say I couldn't guarantee how long those boys would remain healthy."

"I'll healthy you, you!—" shouted Tom, lunging across the counter. With a sweeping motion of his arm, Mullins knocked over the lamp, intending to plunge the room into darkness. Instead, it hit the floor with a crash and spread a pool of fire over the wood floor.

Reaching under the counter, the shopkeeper yanked out a .44 caliber Derringer. Tom, who was sprawled across the counter, rolled to the side, but not before Mullins' shot took him on the side of the head. Tom rolled heavily to the floor and lay still. Mullins paused only long enough to sweep the cuff links into his fist before lumbering heavily out the front door of the store.

The stirring sounds of the community told him that the gunshot had not gone unnoticed. Cursing to himself and moving as rapidly as his bulk permitted, he made his way home to where his buggy was already hitched up and waiting. On the way out of town, he noted grimly that flames could be seen through the store windows, and as he rounded a curve shutting out the view, he heard the church bell begin to give the alarm. "I hope he fries," he muttered as he drove off.

———

Tom was dragged from the fire by the hotel proprietor, McKenna. Ignoring the frantic activity of men scurrying about trying to save the building, he noted that Tom was still alive. The wound, which had knocked him unconscious, had just grazed the side of his head. McKenna and Parson Swift carried Tom to the parson's home, as it was nearer than the hotel. The parson's wife held a cold compress to Tom's head, and soon the wound stopped bleeding.

Tom began to come around as Mrs. Swift bathed his face with cool water, and all at once he gave a jerk and cried out "Mullins! He!—"

"Easy, Tom," urged the parson. "You've been shot, so lie still and rest."

Tom gathered his wits and then spoke again. "Did Mullins get away? Did someone catch him?"

"Do ye mean to say 'twas him as shot ye, lad?" inquired McKenna. "He hasna been seen by me this night. Have ye seen him, Parson?"

"No, but give the man a chance to tell us what he means, Mr. McKenna."

"To be sure," agreed the Scotsman. "Just take yer time, lad, an' tell us what this is all aboot."

Tom opened his eyes, then grimaced in pain and shut them again. Slowly, through gritted teeth he gasped, "Mullins . . . rebel spy, or . . . something. He and Byrd. Got the boys. Killed my brother. Got to follow." As if even this effort was too taxing for his battered brain, Tom fell unconscious again.

Parson Swift looked at McKenna. "Go get Deputy Pettibone, would you, please, Mr. McKenna. I think he should hear this when Tom is able to speak."

"Ay, ay," agreed McKenna. "An' there'll be some others who'll take an interest in his tale as well, I'm thinkin'."

Robert Mullins' mind was whirling faster than the buggy wheels were turning. His first thoughts were of escape only. If he stayed behind, there would be questions—too many questions. How did the fire start? How did Tom Dawson come to be there, shot in the head? Mullins wondered briefly if he could have convinced the town that Dawson was a burglar surprised in the act of rifling the store's safe. But no, no one would believe that. What if Dawson lived?

Mullins knew his bullet had struck Dawson, for the storekeeper had seen him fall heavily to the floor; but in his bolt for the door, Mullins hadn't even considered stopping to see if the man was dead. Cursing his panic,

Mullins thought, *If the man is truly dead, then perhaps I could have sold the burglar idea. Well, no chance of that now. But what if Dawson lives and tells what happened?*

That thought made Mullins snap the reins on the back of his horse and push him to greater speed. What must be done now was a desperate gamble. He must go instantly to Baker's home. The papers must be there; they *must*! Then he remembered the gold stored in the tunnel from the stage robberies in anticipation of the arms purchases. Right now, no one was pursuing him, but that fact might soon change. He might not be able to get back to Shadow Ridge to get the gold. Better to retrieve the gold first, then go and get the papers. He'd take Byrd from the cave as a guard, pick up Yancey at Baker's. Those two could be used to create a diversion if need be, or he could sacrifice them to fight his way clear. Even if he just delivered the gold to the Confederacy, he'd still be a hero, be recognized, be given his rightful place of honor. And, he reasoned, he needn't deliver all the gold. Some of it would compensate him for the loss of his store and his home in Greenville. Maybe there was a way to avoid paying Byrd and Yancey, too. He'd have to think about that.

And what about those two rats in the cave? Too much trouble to take along. And if the papers weren't at Baker's? If the Negro child wasn't telling all he knew? There was still the gold. And the two boys? Leave them tied up in the cave to starve? No, it would be better just to kill them now. The end result was the same anyway, but with no chance of their escaping or being found. Yes, that was all of it. Leave no loose ends. Get the gold, dispose of the two witnesses, go to Baker's, if only briefly, then move on to . . . to where? San Francisco. Of course!

He'd have no difficulty hiding in that booming town. Surely he could find someone to contact, even without the papers. But to live in luxury—ah, that had an attraction all its own.

Mullins had already reached the bend of the road marked by a big oak tree with a huge bare limb that protruded some fifteen feet above the ground. The hanging tree, it was called. Mullins pulled off the road onto a patch of rocky ground. He got out of the buggy and led the horse down a depression bordering Poso Creek and around some brush to a point out of sight of the road.

He retrieved a lantern from the buggy and lit it. Tying the horse to a fallen tree, Mullins clambered awkwardly over it and climbed a steep bank to where some elderberry bushes grew up in front of an overhanging rock. At one time a stream had flowed here, but its course had since shifted underground to join the Poso at a lower point, leaving this concealed tunnel entrance.

Some years ago Mullins had discovered this connection with the summit of Shadow Ridge and all the useful caves and passages in between. Actually, Byrd Guidett had located the upper opening on some occasion when he was fleeing from the law; but after a conversation with Tommy Fitzgerald, Mullins himself had explored the depths of the cave and come upon the lower exit exactly where it was most needed. By leaving his horse at the top of Shadow Ridge, walking downward through the passage and picking up a previously arranged fresh mount here near the road, a man could cut a full day's travel off riding around the circumference of the peak— the way the roads actually went.

Mullins had carefully cultivated the notion that the mountain was haunted, that it was dangerous, that it was impassable. So far these stories and the natural bar-renness of the western slope, together with the difficulty of climbing the eastern approach, had kept the moun-tain's secrets intact. Once or twice it had been necessary for some unfortunately curious folk to get "lost" or have "accidents," but until Jesse Dawson, no one had tried to ignore the danger and live right beside old Shadow. Well, Jesse had been rewarded for his curiosity, all right; maybe now Tom Dawson had been taken care of, too.

Byrd Guidett threw his canteen down in disgust. *Cold water and cold beans! I'm sick of this waitin' around here. There's more blue-bellied Yankees hereabouts than fleas on a dog's back*—he paused to scratch vigorously. *Or on me! An' for what? What if them papers ain't even in this here Baker's house? What if he don't know what I'm after? What if he tries to save his own skin by turnin' me in?*

Each round of Byrd's thoughts grew more and more angry. "An' even if I get them papers," he muttered, "Mul-lins'll jest take 'em without so much as a say. An' he'll be takin' the gold to spend on guns, which he'll try an' give to them crackers up in the hills. Huh! More'n likely they'll turn 'em on him! General Mullins! Governor Mul-lins! What a laugh!"

"Now that gold! In the jobs we already pulled there must be . . ." His shifty eyes got a faraway look, and he squinted up at the sky. "Thar must be close on a hundred thousand dollars! Man, I could live like a king in Frisco with that!"

The thought was more than he could stand. "What do I care who wins the war? I ain't seen 'em hang no medals on me, but if I stick around that fat fool Mullins, they'll be hangin' somethin' else!" He jumped to his feet.

"I'm for the gold," he declared to his horse, "an' right now!"

CHAPTER 19

Tom shook his head and tried to clear it. He sat up, over the protests of the parson and McKenna, and put one hand up to his now-bandaged skull. "Mullins. Did you catch him?"

"Na, lad, he's nae been seen, but the deputy is here now. Do ye feel able to tell him yer tale?"

Tom was able to repeat his story to Pettibone, giving more details about the cuff links. The deputy listened, his eyes wide with astonishment. As Tom recovered somewhat from the grazing wound, his explanation became clearer and all the pieces of the confusing puzzle fell into place.

"Then you believe Mullins masterminded the scheme to hold up the stages and use the gold for some plot?"

"Yes, but something got fouled up when Byrd killed that stranger. The only thing I can figure is that the dead man had something Mullins needed, so he had Byrd kidnap Mont to see if the child knew anything about it. He must think that whatever it is could be hidden in Colonel Baker's home, 'cause that's what I overheard him mumbling about tonight. He's bound to be desperate, because he must know that Baker's being guarded by the army."

Tom paused, and though he sat silently thinking, no

one interrupted to voice an opinion. Finally, he began again. "That means that the boys, if they are still alive now, are in terrible danger. Mullins must have decided that they are no longer needed. Anyway, we can't delay. We've got to follow Mullins right away if the boys are to have any chance at all."

"But follow him where?" asked Pettibone. "We don't know which direction he went out of town, or if he's goin' straight to Baker's, or where his hideout is."

"Yes, we do! Don't you get it? Mullins kept you from searching Shadow Ridge for Guidett right after the killing at Granite. My brother was killed up there when we went looking for a trail, and I don't believe any longer that it was an accident."

"But there is na trail on the Ridge; ye said so yerself," observed McKenna.

"That's right, but there is a cave *under* it! I saw one entrance the day my brother was killed, but I didn't know it for what it was, and afterward I forgot about it till my dream. It must go all the way through and connect up the Tailholt road with this side of the mountain."

"All right, Tom, you've got it ciphered out for sure," said Pettibone. "What'll we do?"

"Parson, you and McKenna should ride to Baker's and alert the soldiers. Have them hold Mullins if he shows up, and get them ready for an attack in case Guidett and some of his kind try to break in."

"Pettibone, take Red and some men and hurry over to Tailholt. When you get there, go up the slope of Shadow. Even if we don't know exactly where that entrance is, they won't be expecting that bolt-hold to be watched, and you can block their escape."

"And what about the lower entrance, Tom—the one

you say you saw on the Poso?" asked the parson.

"I'm counting on Mullins wanting to take his stolen gold with him. He must be going up that way right now. I'm going in after him."

Tom held up his hands to silence their protests. "There aren't enough of us to go around, and we've got to cover the other possibilities in case I'm wrong. But after all he's done to my family . . . just leave him to me; he's my meat."

"Death come aknockin' on dat gambler's door; said, 'O Gambler, are you ready to go?' " sang Mont.

"He said, 'No, no, no, no, no, 'cause I ain't got on my travelin' shoes," responded Nathan enthusiastically.

Neither boy heard the snorting and rustling sounds coming from the other cavern.

"Said, 'O Liar, are ya ready to go?' "

Even louder this time Nathan replied, "No, no, no, no, NO!"

An animal sound went unheard. If either boy had noticed, it would have reminded them of a hawk's diving screech as he swoops to kill.

"O Sinner, are ya ready to go?"

"No, no, no, no—AHHHH!"

The abrupt end to the song and the drawn-out scream from Nathan were caused by Yancey's sudden appearance in the entrance to the prison cave. His eyes were sunken and red-rimmed, which by contrast with his normally ashen skin color made his face appear skull-like. He had his boot knife in his hand and he moved it across in front of his body in slow, downward stabbing arcs.

His words, when they could be understood at all, were slurred and crazy. "No. NO! It won't take me. No! Jest one small death will do."

"Mistuh Yancey, we din't hear you. We'll be quiet now. You—"

"Run, Mont!" yelled Nathan. "He's plumb crazy!"

As if to punctuate Nathan's words, Yancey turned one of his stabbing motions into an outward flip of his wrist. Had not Nathan jerked Mont aside at that instant, Yancey's knife would have been imbedded in the black boy's chest. As it was, it bounced ringing off the rock wall.

"Come on, Mont!" Nathan yelled again, and the two made a dash past Yancey toward the passage. Yancey lunged at them as they went by, catching Nathan by the shirt collar. Nathan twisted in his grasp, crying, "Lemme go! Lemme go!"

Holding the strangling Nathan up by the throat, Yancey twisted the boy around so that they were at eye level. Yancey reached behind his collar with his free hand to draw the other knife that hung there.

Before the man had completely drawn it from its sheath, Mont threw himself at Yancey's legs, and all three tumbled down together. Yancey's cry rose again to a screech, "I've got two for you. Two! Not me; I ain't ready. But here, come and take these!"

Mont scrambled up on the man's chest and flung himself on the arm holding the knife. "Let 'im go! Nathan! Nathan!"

Nathan broke free from Yancey's clutch and struck the outlaw in the face as hard as he could with his two hands doubled together. He and Mont jumped up and dashed into the other cavern.

"Which way'll we go?" cried Nathan.

"Grab de lamp!" yelled Mont, "an' le's go down befo' he can get another light."

Snatching the lamp from the table, the boys jumped into the opening that led to the downward passage, just as Yancey picked himself up and came out the tunnel after them. He threw himself across the table at Nathan, but missed him and sprawled across its top.

Down the boys plunged, on a steeply slanted narrow rock path. Here the floor was slick with moisture coming from the nearby underground stream. With no time to pick their way, the boys skidded around corners and slammed into rocks. From behind them they could hear a keening sound: "I'll find 'em for ya. Just you wait here a spell. I'll bring 'em back."

They came to a place where the tunnel branched. One fork led downward, the other crossed the stream and went upward again. "What'll we do now?" asked Nathan. "He's still followin' us, like he can see in the dark!"

"No, dat ain't it," replied Mont. "He's jes' done dis trip enough so's he knows de way. But he can't foller de other path in de dark. Le's go up!"

The two plunged into the stream. It was icy cold and swifter than they expected. In an instant they were spun around. Mont collided with Nathan and both juggled frantically with the bobbing lamp. It fell against a boulder with a crash and was immediately extinguished.

Nathan jumped for the other bank and was rewarded with a handhold on the far side. Pulling himself up from the water, he turned and offered his hand to Mont. Mont climbed out on the bank, and they began crawling farther into the tunnel, judging their direction just by the upward feel. Behind them they could hear the water rushing down the narrow bed, but above that they could still make out Yancey's strange crooning monologue: "It won't be long now. Oh no, 'most any minute we'll be aknockin' on their door . . . knockin' on their door. Will they be ready? Le's go see, le's go see."

As the crying voice came closer, it was all they could do to lie still in the absolute darkness. Both boys were afraid that Yancey would decide to cross the stream. Nathan and Mont hugged each other and trembled with fear and cold.

———————

Robert Mullins bustled up the tunnel. His thoughts were all of gold and San Francisco, of opulent comfort, culture, and attentive service. Every few steps he paused to wheeze at the labor of the climb up inside the mountain; then he resumed a panting pace, impatient now that his mind was made up to get his hands on the wealth stockpiled there.

He was sweating, partly with exertion and partly with the flush of anticipation. He'd decided that he could convince Byrd that it was time to transport the gold to buy arms; and after enlisting Byrd's help in loading the gold into Mullins' buggy, he'd make off with all of it. With a smile he patted his huge belly at the top of his trousers. Abruptly his smile faded as the handle of the pistol he expected to feel wasn't there. He tried to remember what he had done with the Derringer after shooting Tom. He could have sworn he'd thrust it into his waistband. Frantically he patted his vest and trouser pockets, then, with a relieved sigh, his outside coat pocket. There was the pistol. Mullins recalled that the thought of climbing over the rocks at the cave's mouth with a loaded pistol bound against his gut had made him uneasy, so he had transferred the small weapon to the deep pocket on the outside of his coat. He drew it out to examine it in the lamplight and remembered that he had fired one of its two shots but hadn't reloaded it. "Better safe than sorry," he muttered, and his pudgy fingers squirmed into a vest watch pocket until closing on another .44 cartridge. He broke open the breech and, discarding the spent casing, replaced it with the new one before returning the gun to his coat pocket.

The next part of his hike was Mullins' least favorite, for it involved his girth in a most unpleasant way. The passage he was in continued on past a crevice in the floor some hundred feet farther before coming to a dead-end. The true route lay down through the opening in the floor of the tunnel. A short drop would land him in another parallel passage, from which the journey up continued. A limestone ledge was only four feet below, but the process involved setting down the lantern, fitting himself into the opening and groping with his feet for the ledge. There he could stand and retrieve the lamp before stepping on down another three feet to the passage floor.

He put the lantern down close to the edge and eased himself into the opening. His small feet began pawing at the rock in search of the ledge as his weight transferred to his arms. The moment's effort made him puff, but his toes located the spot and he moved to grasp the lamp and continue down. But he couldn't move. He had grown so fat that, with the addition of the heavy coat and the presence of the Derringer pushing against his hip, he was unable to slide any farther down. Standing on his boot tips, he tried to raise himself back up to the space above, but his arms could not support his poundage and overcome the friction of the tight fit. With his arms stuck above the hole and his legs straining sideways to maintain contact with the small ledge, he made a most effective cork in a bottle.

———————

"Where did ya go, little travelers? Come out and meet a friend," crooned Yancey. "Are ya ready to go?"

He scraped on down the tunnel, past the side branch that the boys had chosen as a hiding place. Feeling his way along the limestone passage, he slowly waved his knife back and forth in front of him. Occasionally he would rub it against his shirt sleeve as if wiping it clean of blood.

He came to a place where the passage widened out and then split into a maze of smaller channels woven among a thicket of limestone columns that reached up to the roof. For some reason, Yancey decided that the boys were playing hide-and-seek with him in this room, so he began to creep softly around each corner, thrusting ahead of him with the knife. He lowered his monologue to a whisper, but continued chanting, "No, no, no, no, ain't ready to go, 'cause I ain't got on my travelin' shoes."

Nathan and Mont were petrified. They had heard Yancey pass their escape route and could not bear the thought of his attempting to cross over. They feared that they could not cross the stream again without making so much noise that he would hear and return to catch them, so they decided to crawl farther into the side tunnel and hope for a way out.

Mont crawled in front, with Nathan coming along behind, one hand grasping Mont's ankle. They stayed down on all fours because in the total blackness they were afraid that they would fall over an unseen drop-off.

After crawling some distance, they felt rather than saw the passage widen around them. They had reached another good-sized room, but had no way of guessing its extent, the height of the roof, or where it led.

"What if we're crawlin' straight for a dead-end?" whispered Nathan.

"Does you want to go back?" returned Mont over his shoulder.

Nathan thought about the tunnel they had left behind with Yancey and his knife and shuddered. "No!" he whispered urgently. "Only, let's get on out of here." Then he added, "Please, God!"

To which Mont just as fervently replied a whispered "Amen!"

Mont put out his hand to move a bit farther and drew it back in horror. "Nathan!" he breathed, "dey's a dead body here! Ah can feel his trousers, an' his leg is cold an' stiff!"

Nathan jerked backward and wanted desperately to run, but a supreme effort made him hold still, deciding that a dead body was less of a threat than a live Yancey. "Are you sure?" he asked.

"Well, ah thinks I is. Here's his one leg an' here's another. My, dey do feel hard!" Gritting his teeth, Mont gingerly knocked his knuckles against the leg.

"Whooee!" he breathed. "It ain't a dead man; it's jes' a pile of sacks or somethin'."

"Sacks?" whispered Nathan, curious in spite of the recent scare. "What would a heap of sacks be doin' here?" He crawled up past Mont's side and reached out to touch the objects in front of them. "You're right. It's a whole mess of canvas bags. What do you suppose is in 'em?"

With these words he began to poke around the sacks, feeling the heavy oblong objects contained in them. After a moment's thought, he said excitedly, "Mont, it's the gold—the stolen gold! This here is the loot stolen from the stage holdups. I bet there's even a reward for findin' this!"

When Mont made no comment to share his friend's enthusiasm, Nathan asked, "What's the matter, Mont, ain't this excitin'?"

"Nathan, it's *too* excitin'! Don'cha see? Dis here is de gang's loot! Dis ain't no secret tunnel; dey knows jes' where it is. An' sooner or later, dey's gonna think to look here!"

CHAPTER 20

"Wal, wal, what have we got here? An ol' hog stuck in a gate? My, don't he squeal!"

"Byrd, thank God you're here. I'm stuck in this cursed hole. Pull me up, and be quick about it!"

"Now hold on a mite. I seen yer buggy asettin' down to the bottom. You musta come here in the middle of the night. That ain't like you fat boys, what likes yer soft beds. Now, why d'ya s'pose a fine citizen like ol' Robert Mullins'd be out here this time of night?"

"Pull me out!" Mullins swore at Byrd, but could move neither up nor down.

"Tut, tut! Such speech to be acomin' from a church-goin' feller." Byrd was clearly enjoying Mullins' predic-ament, and the storekeeper was about to be overcome with rage when a thought struck him.

"Why are you coming from outside the cave? Where's Yancey? Why aren't you guarding those two brats? And who's watching Baker's house? Baker's," he said again. "Did you get the papers? Is that why you're here?"

"Naw," replied Byrd with a grin. "I'm here for the same reason as you, I reckon. I been wet, an' I been cold, but I ain't agonna be poor much longer."

Mullins suddenly shivered all over. "You've got it all

231

wrong, Byrd," he soothed. "I was coming up here to divide the gold with all three of us. Yes, that's what I came here for."

"Ain't that mighty white of you, General Mullins? Wal', the way I figgers, two shares is better'n three. An' one is even better yet. Ain't that the way you got it figgered?"

Before Mullins could utter a word of protest or plea, Byrd drew his Walker and shot Robert Mullins between the eyes. Mullins feet slipped from the ledge and the weight of his body caused him to fall heavily through the opening.

"Ain't that somethin'?" remarked Byrd wonderingly. "He weren't really stuck any of the time."

"We are climbin' Jacob's ladder," crooned Yancey, "sol'jers of the cross." Around the maze of limestone byways he glided, stabbing his knife into corners and into side passageways before entering them himself.

"Climbin' Jacob's ladder, gonna climb them golden stairs. Golden stairs," he repeated. "Gonna climb right up to the sun. All kindsa light up on that golden stair."

"Gold," he repeated. "Up the ladder to the gold."

"My, my, my," he said, a crafty grin playing over his features, "what have we got here? Lights to light the night, right on up the golden ladder."

So saying, he produced a box of matches from his pants' pocket, which his fever-ridden brain had not remembered till now.

Striking one, he turned about to face back up toward the passage he had just descended and sang to himself, "Are ya ready to go? They said, 'No, no, no, no, no . . .' "

––––––––––

Tom halted Duncan beside Mullins' buggy and Byrd's horse. Not knowing exactly where to look along the banks of Poso Creek for the tunnel entrance he expected to find, Tom had ridden slowly along the road. His pace had been much quieter than Byrd's pounding ride, so it was easy to get off the road to watch without being spotted. Tom didn't know Byrd for who he was, but he reasoned that few people up to any good would be out in the middle of the night, and fewer still would have a reason to turn off at this spot.

He had allowed Duncan his head, and the canny horse, like a huge bloodhound, had followed Byrd's track as it wound down to the stream bed. Tom had watched as Byrd lit a lantern and climbed up and into the entrance to the cave. What with Mullins having such a long head start, Tom had been convinced that to tackle the unknown rider would delay him further or in some way warn the fleeing storekeeper.

Now Tom tried to decide what to do next. He thought briefly of returning to town for help since his idea was correct and he had run Mullins to earth, but he was afraid they might leave before he could return. He also couldn't stand the thought of the boys being held captive one moment longer. Tom waited a couple of minutes; then taking a bull's-eye lantern from a saddlebag, he lit it and proceeded to enter the cave.

Just inside the tunnel mouth, he heard a gunshot. Tom's heart sank. "Oh, God," he prayed, "let the boys be all right! Don't let me come this close and not rescue them."

He carried his lantern in his left hand and his Colt

in his right. Even though his lantern might betray his presence, Tom hoped that anyone he might encounter would not be climbing around this secret place with his weapon at the ready; so he felt he would have the advantage.

Now his insides were twisting. He didn't know whether he should run ahead toward the sound of the shot or continue his cautious stalk. When no further shots were fired, and no other sounds indicated another person's location, Tom decided to continue moving quietly.

Up ahead, just around a bend of the tunnel, he suddenly saw a light. Tom dropped to a crouch. Setting his own lantern down behind him, he drew as far over to the other wall of the passage as possible, keeping close to the shadows and advancing with the Colt leading the way. Carefully he peered around a corner.

He saw Mullins' lantern still sitting in the middle of the cavern floor. Tom wondered if it could be a trap. Reaching down with his left hand, he picked up a small chunk of quartz. Preparing himself to fight, he hurled the rock at the lamp. He missed, but the resulting clatter sounded as loud as an avalanche to his ears. When nothing happened and no one appeared, Tom decided to chance going on forward. He slowly approached the crevice, scanning all around as he did so.

After another quick glance around, Tom looked downward into the opening. There lay Robert Mullins, his jowls sagging limply. He seemed to have grown a third eye in his forehead. Tom guessed at what had transpired, but wasted no more thoughts on Robert Mullins. Instead, he made a quick examination of the hole and spotted the ledge for stepping down. He swung his legs into the opening, aware that he was going to be completely helpless for a moment. With this thought, he skipped stepping to the ledge, but allowed himself to drop through the hole in one motion, just missing Mullins' body as he did so.

Almost without thinking, he bent and scooped up the Derringer that had fallen from Mullins' pocket, and thrust it through his belt. Looking around quickly, Tom guessed that he would have already drawn a shot if there were a sentry, so he stepped back up onto the ledge and retrieved the lamp from beside the hole. He then proceeded to advance up the passage as before.

"Oh, Gambler, are ya ready to go? Go up Jacob's ladder?" Yancey was moving rapidly back up the tunnel, striking matches as he went and walking quickly with the help of the light. He moved purposefully now, his knife carried blade upward in his fighting stance. No longer did he wave it around or stab it into corners. He clearly had a destination in mind, and he was heading there.

The boys had climbed over the sacks of gold, reasoning that the best they could do now was to try to get still deeper into the side passage. They were still crawling, but now Nathan was leading. Mont was praying aloud, "Oh, Jesus, he'p us, Jesus, he'p us get outta here."

Byrd could hear some sounds up ahead of him, but he couldn't quite make out the words. "Blast!" he said, drawing his Walker, "what in blazes is goin' on up here?"

"Yancey?" he called out. "Yancey, is that you? Where are ya?"

Yancey stopped lighting matches as he heard Byrd's

yell. He had just reached the point at which the side tunnel branched off to reach the gold. Yancey lit one more in order to get his bearings; then he stepped into the stream and crossed over. Just on the other side he stopped, his back pressed against the wall of the passage and waited. "Death come aknockin' on that sinner's door," he muttered.

Upward went Byrd. He noticed the trail of burned-out matches. "Those kids musta run off, an' Yancey's tryin' to find 'em. Why ain't he got a lantern, though?"

When Byrd reached the side tunnel, he raised his lantern high over his head so as to illuminate the far bank. Sure enough, he could just make out the wet tracks where someone had crossed. "Yancey!" he yelled, "C'mon back out here, an' we'll hunt 'em together. C'mon, ya cussed snake, I ain't gettin' my feet wet less'n ya tell me what's up!"

There was no reply. "You don't s'pose ol' Yancey got to hankerin' after that gold hisself?" mused Byrd aloud. "You cain't trust nobody!" As he stepped into the stream, he saw a flash reflected from Yancey's knife as Yancey lunged from the shadows. Byrd's foot turned on a rock, his sideways sprawl saving him. Yancey's thrust was intended to catch Byrd in the stomach just as he emerged from the crossing, but instead it caught only air.

Byrd's revolver leaped into his hand, and he fired. Byrd saw the first bullet strike Yancey, but in twisting around and firing, Byrd dropped his lantern into the water. He fired twice more in quick succession—once into the body he saw starting to topple and once more into the blackness of the floor where he believed Yancey to be.

All was still. "Yancey?" Byrd called softly. "I sure

hope you is dead, but if ya ain't you better talk nice an' sweet to me less'n my finger gets to jumpin' again." There was no reply—not even a groan. "I reckon I'm done with you," he concluded, pulling himself up out of the water. Carefully he kicked Yancey's body, holding his Walker ready. He kicked again—harder this time.

"Yup. I don't know what got inta ya, but I figgered it'd end thisaway anyhow, iff'n that's any comfort to ya."

He rummaged through the corpse's pockets till he found the matches. "Jest a handful left? I guess ya won't be needin' 'em, ol' cuss, so I'll jest mosey along an' check on my gold."

The boys froze at the sounds coming from the tunnel behind them; they heard Byrd's yell echo down the passage. "We'll hunt 'em together." When the shots came, the boys didn't know what to make of it. They waited silently, hearts pounding like a blacksmith's hammers as they waited to see what would happen next.

Back toward the sacks of gold they peered, straining to see something through the darkness. Presently they could see a flicker of light, and once they heard Byrd swear as he held a match too long and burned himself. They saw him illuminated in the scratching hiss of another match as he crouched over the gold, his face an evil mask of gloating delight, made hideous by the strange play of shadows around his beard.

Nathan gave an involuntary gasp, and instantly clapped his hand over his mouth. But Byrd had heard. He looked into the darkness where they lay and called out, "Is you kids there? Come on out. I ain't gonna hurt ya. Yancey done went crazy, but I've fixed him, an' the ol' fat boy, too. Come on out now, I say."

When neither child moved or uttered another word,

Byrd gave an exasperated sigh. "You'uns is determined to make this tough, ain't ya?" He shook out the match and lit another while counting to himself. "Lessee, one bullet for Mullins an' three for Yancey. Why, that leaves me jest enough, don't it?"

"Don't count on it," said a voice from behind him. Hearing the gunshots, Tom had blown out his lantern and had been watching as Byrd crossed the stream, following by the flashes of Byrd's matches. He had arrived just in time.

Byrd whirled, dropping the match and plunging the cave into darkness as he did so. He fired a shot in the direction from which Tom's voice had come, then threw himself to the floor of the cavern and found shelter behind the gold. His bullet caught Tom's gun barrel and spun the revolver out of Tom's grasp.

"Whyn't ya shoot, Dawson? Could it be I've killed ya jest like we did yer brother? Like I'm fixin' to do with them two brats?"

Byrd reached into his pocket and drew out another match. Holding his cocked pistol across the canvas sacks, he struck the match on the cave's floor and held it aloft in his left hand.

Lying just a few feet away was Tom. Byrd noticed the shattered Colt Navy lying against the far wall and the bandages swathing Tom's head. "Why, shoot, Dawson," said Byrd, rising to his feet, "you was 'most dead already. But, since I got this here bullet, I'll use it on you, an' then I'll take care of yer brats. An' then," he added, leering, "I aim to pay a little visit to that Emily lady."

At these words, Nathan rose up behind Byrd, shouting, "No! no! You can't hurt my ma!"

"What the—?" was all Byrd got out of his mouth

before Tom snatched the Derringer from his belt and put a .44 slug straight through Byrd Guidett's heart.

"Keep still, boys," called Tom. "Let's wait to see that this isn't a trick."

A moment later he called, "Say, where's that light coming from?" A faint silvery glow was coming from the far end of the tunnel. By it, Tom could see Nathan and Mont come out of their concealment, and could make out Byrd's body slumped over the sacks of gold.

"Uncle, Uncle! Mistuh Tom!" came the glad cries as the boys ran to Tom.

After a moment of embracing, Tom observed, "That's got to be daylight, boys. Let's go see where it leads."

Around the next corner, the boys drew up against Tom in sudden alarm. Daylight was pouring into the cave through a hole in the roof, and lying at the bottom of a ramp of dirt leading up and out was the skull of Tommy Fitzgerald's gigantic grizzly.

Tom laughed as he hugged the two boys again, and putting his arms around the boys' shoulders, he climbed up the incline to stand in the morning light. He stood looking down the eastern slope of Shadow Ridge toward where the ranch and Emily were waiting. "Come on, boys," he said. "Let's go home!"